BAD GIRL

A collection of erotic stories

Alison Tyler

Published by Accent Press Ltd – 2008
ISBN 9781906125806

Printed and bound in the UK

Cover Design by
Red Dot Design

For SAM
Always

Also available from Xcite Books:

www.xcitebooks.com

Contents

To Lola, With Love

I'm not exactly sure how to admit this – it sounds funny to say, and looks funnier on paper – but my girlfriend is having an affair with my vagina. She'll readily admit to it. She's even written love letters to it. Yes, indeed, Jo, my normally sane, very lovely, dyke-sweetheart has taken pen in hand and written to my cunt.

At first, she simply cooed to it, sliding one deft pointer between my nether lips, then lifting that finger to her mouth to drink the nectar from the tip, whispering softly, "Oooh, pretty thing, pretty pussy. Oooh, what darling kitty lips you have. I'm gonna lick 'em. Yesss, I am. I'm gonna drink all that sticky sap from deep inside. Oh, yes, darlin', oh yes."

She employed the exact same voice that some slightly deranged people use when talking to babies or small animals. That sing-song, nonsense tone. That wuvvy-duvvy, cartoonish croon. That nausea-inspiring simper that suggests the very early stages of puppy love.

But this love has lasted.

And so has the love affair Jo has held with my vagina.

Now, she's not totally off the deep end. I mean, she hasn't proposed marriage to it or anything. But she brings it presents.

"Won't you look pretty in these satin panties?" she

crows. "Oh, yes, oh yes, so pretty for Mommy…"

Excuse me?

"Mama Jo got them special. See the lace, pretty lace…"

Okay, she's talking to my cunt, I thought, at first. *I can handle this. I can get a grip.* Except, she was talking to it as if it had the brain of, say, Jell-O. So, I came to a decision: if my cunt is gonna have a love affair behind my back – no, that's impossible – *in front of* my back, then it had better get treated with some respect. I wanted intelligent conversation, not baby doll cooing. And I told her so.

"None of your business, really," is what Jo had to say.

"Excuse me?"

"It's none of your business what Lola and I do, or how we talk."

"Lola?"

"Yes, that's her name."

"*You named my cunt*?"

"No… she told me."

Too much. Too fucking much.

"My cunt *told* you her name?"

"Well," Jo said, shrugging her built shoulders at me and giving me a withering stare, "Not in so many words, but I knew."

I didn't have anything to say to that. Not at first, anyway. I told myself that perhaps I was just being naive. I'd only been in one long-term relationship before Jo, and that was with a girl even shyer than me. Maybe normal couples talked to each others pussies every day. Maybe I was overreacting. But, still, waking up to Jo saying, "Good morning, Lola," was a little hard to get used to. I mean, Lola didn't have to go to work. Lola didn't want fresh coffee. Lola was just fine sleeping late. Didn't Jo want to wish *me* a good morning? I was, after all, the one who ironed her work clothes. Who ran out for bagels and the Sunday paper. Lola couldn't do any of that.

Finally, I decided to discuss the situation with my best friend. Katy wasn't the least bit sympathetic. She said I should be happy, that I should be pleased with all the attention I was getting. The love letters written on the bathroom mirror. The presents. She said that I should count my blessings and think of all the lonely-hearted dykes out there who don't have gorgeous girlfriends wanting to make love to them all the time.

"But she talks to it," I said.

"So?" Katy asked me. "Don't you ever talk to yourself? Talk to your computer? People talk to their cars, even. It's not so strange." Katy paused. "What would be strange is if Lola talked back." She paused again, thoughtfully. "There's a ventriloquist act I wouldn't mind catching."

"She named it," I told her, even though that was one of the things I wasn't sure I was going to reveal. There are some pieces of information people should probably keep to themselves. But I know enough of Katy's secrets that I was sure mine would be safe with her.

And Katy saw no problem with this little tidbit either. "Guys name theirs all the time. Mr Happy. Little Willie. Big Johnson. Hairy Larry."

"How would you know about what guys do?" I asked.

"I got brothers," Katy said. "I hear things."

"Anyway," I told her, indignantly, "*I* didn't give it a name. She did. Lola wouldn't even have been in my top ten list."

"Lovers give each other pet names all the time," Katy said. "Remember how Grace used to call me Puddytat."

"And it drove you mad," I reminded her, mimicking

Grace and the way she'd say, "I tawt I taw a Puddytat. Plus," I pointed out, "Jo's not calling *me* Lola. She's calling my pussy Lola."

"Well, why don't you name her cooch? Let her see what it feels like?"

I considered it. I pictured a naked Jo standing in front of me, called up a mental image of her full-figured body, and the strip of fuzz she shaves Mohawk-style, covering the lips of her pussy. The only name that came to my mind was Chuck. Don't ask me why. Maybe the shortness of her hair made me think of an airforce lieutenant I once met at a bar. I could just imagine how well that nickname would go over. No, beating Jo at her own game wasn't going to work.

"Any other ideas?" I asked Katy. She was less than helpful.

"I just don't see what the big deal is," Katy told me. "You've got a girlfriend who loves you more than anything. Who pampers you and plays with you. Who's gone so far as to make up nicknames for your body parts. Why are you trying to make problems where there aren't any? Are you one of those women who's simply never satisfied?"

"No," I said, honestly. "I'm more than satisfied."

"Does she call you from work, make you put Lola on the phone?"

I shook my head.

"Has she asked to be alone with Lola?"

I hesitated, unsure about whether I was ready to confess the rest of it. But with her staring at me like that, waiting, practically daring me, I said in a low voice, so nobody else in the cafe could hear, "She asked her to dance."

This made Katy laugh out loud. "There's a vision,"

she said, enthralled. "Did she get down on the floor, first? Right down there on her knees in the sawdust? Did she look at Lola eye-to-eye? Or, mouth to mouth? Or, really, lips to lips?"

I shook my head.

"Come on," Katy said, "All dancing is about sex. Body parts pressed up against body parts. It's just a form of publicly accepted foreplay. With you and Jo, the end results were going to be the same. You'd be in bed together by the end of the evening whether you danced with her or not. What's the difference whether she asked your whole self to dance or just your cunt?"

"This wasn't the hokey-pokey. You put your pussy in. You put your pussy out. You put your pussy in and you shake it all about." I told her. "This was me and Jo, at a bar. On one of our little dates."

"Give it a break," Katy said. "Your girlfriend wanted to dance with you. There's nothing abnormal about that at all. She's just a bit eccentric in the way she asked."

Which is really all I wanted to hear. Because, in all honesty, I was starting to like the added attention. And the dancing thing had been sort of cute. Sort of sweet in an odd, unbelievable way. It happened after a long day at work, when we decided to relax and go out to Ladies Night. You know, the bar on Fourth Street and Main. Me and Jo were sitting on those tall, wooden chairs and drinking our shots, watching as the fools tried their hand at line dancing. Can you believe they still teach that? Every Thursday from six to seven. But this one night, when the class was over, Jo walked to the jukebox and started slipping in the quarters. And all of a sudden, *The Girl From Ipanema* – our song – poured out of the speakers and there was Jo, standing in front of me, looking me up and down in that way of hers, as if she's adding up a long list of numbers in her head. A list of very large numbers, nodding as if she approves of the total sum.

"Wanna dance–" she asked softly. Before I could give her an answer, which would have been yes, of course, she finished the question, "Wanna dance, Lola?"

"Lola?" I said, surprised.

"Can't I dance with her?" Jo pouted, acting hurt, as if I were depriving her of a great delight by saying no.

"H-How…?" I stammered. Did she want me to get undressed for her at the bar? Slip off my clothes and let her dance with Lola? Jo has asked me to do much odder things than that in our three years together. She's taken my panties away from me during a long car ride, had me spread my legs up on the dashboard and let her watch while I've pleasured myself. At her insistence, we joined the mile high club. The mile low club on the Chunnel when we took a vacation from London to Paris. We've even joined the yard wide club in the back of my VW bug. What was she asking for now?

"Just trust me," Jo said, "And let me lead." So, against better judgement, I let her. Felt those strong arms come around me, groove me over to the dance floor, position me just right and then move with me. Back and forth. Gyrating. My little body was tight against her larger, more substantial form. And in the heat of it, the dimness of the bar, the sound of the music around us, everything started to make sense.

I swear. With Lola pressed up like that against Jo, the rest of my body simply melted away. I started to realise that there was something about the swing and the sway of it. I started to get into this whole *ménage à trois* thing. This *ménage à trois* for the mind. I could tell Jo was pleased with my behaviour. And I could tell that Lola was feeling pretty enthusiastic, as well. I started to think that maybe Katy was right. What girl wouldn't be happy? Dancing. Presents. Drinks all night at her favourite bar.

And that, I thought, was that.

At least, until Valentine's Day, when the flowers arrived. She'd sent them with a pastel note that read in that gently sloping cursive: "To Lola, with love." For some reason, this pushed me over the edge. Dancing was one thing. Pretty panties were another. But flowers for Lola? Flowers for *her* instead of for me? Sent with love on the most romantic day of the year? I started to feel – I don't know how to say this – but I started to feel left out. But before doing anything truly stupid, I called Katy for advice.

"What is your problem?" she asked.

"She sent Lola flowers."

"Do you know what I got for Valentine's Day?" Katy asked.

Uh oh, I thought. "What?" I asked, hopefully.

"Nothing. Not one thing. Not a card. Not candy. Not a single flower. *You* didn't even send me one of those pathetic girl cards that friends send to their loser friends who don't have Valentines. Do you think I'm the right person you should be talking to?"

"Maybe not," I admitted.

"*I* didn't get flowers. And my cunt didn't get flowers." Katy sighed, then calmed down. A little. "Really, Angel. What exactly is your problem today?"

"She sent the flowers to Lola. Not me."

"How can you be green about your own pussy?" Katy asked. "It's like a topic on the Jerry Springer show. Women Who Are Jealous of Their Vaginas."

"Ha, ha," I said.

"Isn't this like being jealous of an inanimate object?"

Katy continued, "Like those women who are jealous of baseball because their husbands are always watching the game."

"Hey…" I said, not liking the tone of her voice or, to be perfectly honest, the way she was talking about Lola, comparing her to a sport. Really.

"Or of a pet," Katy continued. "Jealous of a dog or a–"

"Pussy?" I interrupted.

"Remember what the Bible says?" Katy asked, switching subjects so fast that she lost me in the change-over.

"No," I said, wondering what in God's name the Bible had to do with any of this.

"Thou shalt not covet thy neighbour's –"

"What?" I asked, interrupting again. "Wife?"

"Something like that," Katy said. "I never paid much attention at Sunday school."

"It just feels as if she's cheating on me," I finally admitted. "It feels as if she's sent flowers to another woman, this Lola woman, and that I found out by accident." I paused. "You know that I caught my ex-girlfriend in bed with someone else. You know how hard it is for me to trust people."

"So you're saying that Jo's committing adultery with your own pussy," Katy said, "Is that right? Have I got all the facts straight?"

"Yeah," I muttered. When she put it like that it sounded ridiculous.

"This is way too confusing for me," Katy said. "I think you'd better talk to Jo. Or get yourself some therapy."

If those were the two choices, I knew which one to pick. So I called Jo at work.

"Seventh Street Cafe," Jo answered, that familiar

smile in her husky voice, "You've reached the bar…"

"Jo, why did you send my cunt flowers?"

"Hey!" she said, "You weren't supposed to open the card, it was for *her*."

"Um, what's 'she' gonna do with them?"

"Smell them. Enjoy them."

"We have to talk," I said.

"Sure, Angel. I'll be home at one."

I paced through the apartment, unable to park myself at the computer and get my work done. I'd started to feel as if sitting were a bad thing… I mean, sitting on *her*. And I suddenly felt the urge to take a bath, to shave Lola cleanly, to stand naked in front of the bouquet so she *could* enjoy them.

I ran the water in our claw-foot tub, adding raspberry-scented bubble bath and lighting a few candles. Normally, I wouldn't get so carried away, but this seemed to be a special occasion – flowers, and all. As I spread on the shaving cream, I found that I touched myself more gently than normal. I slid the razor over that softest skin and admired it. When I was through, I powdered all over, then went and got the pretty panties Jo had bought and put them on.

Lola was happy. I could tell.

Jo came home on schedule, a wrapped present under one arm.

I was sitting on the couch, nude save for the panties; the flowers well within smelling-range on the coffee table.

"For Lola?" I asked, unable to keep the green-eyed monster at bay.

"Naw, cutie, for you."

I felt myself melt, reaching greedily for the gift. Inside, nestled in fluffy tissue paper, lay a silvery dildo and a black leather harness.

"Well," Jo conceded, "Not *only* for you, but for Lola, as well."

"Oh…" I sighed when I saw it, stroking the moulded plastic. I felt a tightness in my chest. I wanted that toy. And, from the response going on down in my panties, Lola wanted it, too.

"Wait in the bedroom," Jo told me. "I think the three of us can work all this out."

"Yeah," I agreed shyly, growing even more damp at the thought of what was in store. "Yeah, I think so, too."

I followed her order, quickly walking through the living room and to our bedroom. I lay on the bed, staring at my reflection in the mirror on the back of our dresser. My cheeks were flushed, my dark eyes on fire. I tossed my glossy raven mane away from my face, feeling the warmth at the back of my neck, beneath my heavy tresses. Every part of my body was growing hot. *Especially* Lola. I waited, impatiently, for Jo to join me – I mean, *us* – and while I did, I snaked one hand under the satin panties and began to stroke Lola.

She was ready, all right. Sticky juices were dripping from her hungry lips. I slid my fingers in and out, getting them wet, then spreading the warm honey all over her shaved skin.

Finally, Jo entered. She had stripped and was wearing the harness and moulded synthetic cock. It stuck out, away from her body, pointing directly at me.

"You *are* jealous, aren't you?" she asked, coming toward the bed so quickly that I didn't notice the handcuffs concealed in one of her large hands.

"I…"

She captured my wrists easily, setting the chain of the cuffs neatly in the hook over our headboard. Now, without having to rush, she fastened my ankles with crimson silk loops and tied them to the posters of our bed.

"Such a jealous girl. Jealous of the attention I've bestowed on your little friend. Why is that, Angel? It doesn't really make much sense."

I couldn't explain.

"I love you, darlin'," Jo said to me, slipping into her slight, South Texas drawl. "I love you desperately. And I love her, as well." She cupped one hand protectively over my cunt. I still had the panties on, and I wondered how she'd get around them. Jo had no problems, though, no worries. She simply reached for a pair of sewing scissors on the dresser and sliced through the filmy material.

"Oh," she sighed, once Lola was revealed, "You shaved." Now she pressed her heart-shaped lips to my nether lips and began to lick, lapping deliciously at the flood of juices that glistened on my cunt, and thighs, and ass. "Yes, you did. You shaved for Mama."

I didn't think it was polite for me to answer, not being directly spoken to. But, I was unable to keep silent.

"I…" I started.

"Yes, Angel?" Jo asked looking up at me. Her chin was glossy with my honey, her lips wet and shiny.

"*I* shaved for you."

That made her smile. "Thank you, Angel. I know you did."

Ah, sanity. Sweet sanity. I saw it once again in my lover's lake green eyes.

"Lola told you that I wanted her to be clean, right?"

"I…" I started again, unsure of how to answer.

"Not in so many words, of course," Jo said, quoting from herself, "But you knew, right?"

I nodded. Yes, I'd known.

"Good. Now lie back, sweetheart, and let Mama go to work."

I had no problem with that. I relaxed against the pillows and closed my eyes. Jo spread Lola's lips with her fingers, and her knowing tongue quickly began making the darting little circles that I love best. She went 'round and 'round with the tip of her tongue, moving away from my clit, then closer to it. I arched my hips, sliding on the crisp white sheets, helping her. I tensed my muscles against the ribbons of fabric that held me in place. I moaned and sighed. I shivered as I got closer to the moment of truth.

Then everything stopped.

I opened my eyes, startled, desperate. Jo was looking back at me, a coy smile on her lips. She sat on her heels, regarding my supine form, then she began to stroke the dildo, just watching me, not saying anything.

I swallowed hard, wanting to beg, but not sure if that would get me anywhere. When Jo has that look in her jewel-toned eyes, that *knowing* look, it means 'watch out'. I stared as she spit into her right palm and began oiling the cock. I stared as she slid her fingers around it, pulling on it, working it. I felt my pussy lips part, I felt the juices trickle through the swollen crack. I was dying.

"Now, listen," Jo said, her voice gone dark and low and sweet, like thick molasses pouring slowly all over my body. "And listen well, child…"

I nodded.

"I love you. Oh, Angel, you know I love you. I see you as a whole: your brain, your heart, your soul, your cunt – all of your parts work together to make up the you that I love. And sometimes, in some phases of our relationship, I've focused on your mind… think back, you know I'm telling the truth." I closed my eyes, considering, and then nodded. She was right. "And sometimes," she continued, and now I could hear the teasing in her voice, "I have courted your heart." I nodded again, knowing now where she was going with this. "And, Angel, there have been phases that I've gone directly for your soul. Am I speaking the truth?"

She waited until I opened my eyes again and said, "Yes, Jo, you are."

"Well, now," she said, still in that low voice, "I am having a love affair with your cunt. I adore her. I want to pamper her, to play with her, to give her everything she needs... like this..." She moved forward, placing the head of the dildo on the flat bone above my pussy. "Just like this, 'cause you need this, and I need this, and Lola needs this."

I leaned my head back against the pillow, my whole body straining. I wanted her IN. I would have agreed to anything as long as she went IN. But she didn't, she just rocked back and forth, taunting me.

"Yes," I finally managed. "Yes, I understand."

"Ah, good... I knew you would."

And with that, she slid down the two inches that she was from paradise and thrust forward, deep, probing me, fucking me – or fucking *her*. And I was no longer jealous, though I did feel as if there were three of us in bed, the way Jo talked, the way she crooned in that syrupy voice, "That's it, doll, that's right," not differentiating between me and Lola, but definitely talking to us both. I could feel the honey flow, coating the moulded cock, making it slick with nectar, and it no longer mattered who was speaking, who was being spoken to.

"Oh, yes," Jo sighed, "Just like that, get it nice and wet for me." Then her hand under my chin, tilting my head forward, "'Cause *you're* gonna suck it clean, right, Angel? You're gonna get it all nice and clean for me."

"Yes," I promised. "Yes, Jo, whatever you say."

"I want you to taste her," Jo said, her eyes gone dreamy, her voice still lost in that soft, commanding tone. "She's so fuckin' sweet."

"Yes, Jo, yesss."

She kept it up, that steady rhythm, the beat I needed, the beat she needed, the beat Lola needed. Kept it up…ragged, desperate, endless. I moaned and writhed, I bucked and screamed, and I got so wet that the bed was a pool of my glossy cum, my thighs dripping with liquid sex. The scent was all around us – we were swimming in it – and I breathed in deep and drank the perfume in, as if I were smelling someone else, some other lover. Everything seemed new to me, taking it from Jo's point of view. I felt newly discovered, newly found out, virginal in a way, and I basked in it, bathed in it… closed my eyes and jumped.

The Lindy Shark

With a blare from the slide trombone, Lilly Faye and her Fire-Spittin' Fellas lit into the first number of the evening. Clara rushed to find her place, her polka-dotted dress swirling about her. Within moments, she was grabbed around the waist, pulled into a tight embrace, twirled fiercely and without finesse, then passed onto the next man in line. This one had thick, meaty fingers that held her too tightly, creasing the fabric of her carefully ironed dress. She was relieved to be released onto the next partner. Her ruffled red panties showed as the third man spun her, dipped her, and passed her on again.

Aside from the briefest of observations, she hardly had time to notice what her partners looked like. Her appraisals were finished with every turn, started fresh with the next. Even when a man did please her, there was no way to move on the interaction. The leader would call out to switch, and she'd be pressed onto the next dancer. Still, she couldn't help but feel a wash of anticipation at the dim prospect that she would be matched with someone who not only suited her moves, but passed her stringent critique system. Although it hadn't happened lately, that didn't mean it couldn't. Maybe *he* would be here again. Perhaps, he would notice her this time.

To the sounds of *Jump, Jive, and Wail*, Clara found

herself with five different men in a row who failed to please her. Handsome, but a poor dancer. Fine-looking, but much too short. Sweaty. A groper. Bad, bad hair. Then, finally, as the leader called out for only the experienced lindy-hoppers to take the floor, she saw him, watched as he moved through the crowd with that insolent look. He had heavy-lidded eyes, a tall, sleek body. Like a shark on the prowl, he cut cleanly through the waves of dancers.

"Fine threads," a woman next to Clara said, staring at the man, as well.

"Racket jacket, pulleys, and a dicer," her friend added.

A little too 'in the lingo', Clara thought as she refocused on her dream man, but the women were right. His vintage zoot suit looked as if it had been made for him, the suspenders flashed when his coat opened, and the fedora added to his high-class appearance. He had an unreadable expression on his face, a steady gaze that almost seemed to look through her. Then he lifted his chin in her direction, letting her know that he had seen her and that he approved.

Of course, he approved, Clara thought. Her sunset-coloured hair, dark red streaked with gold and bronze, was done in pin curls that had taken hours to achieve. She'd applied make-up in the manner of the time, bright matte lips and plenty of mascara. Her vintage dress was navy with white polka-dots, and it cinched in tight on her tiny waist. A pair of stacked heels that were sturdy enough to dance in, but high enough to make those moves look even more complicated than they were, completed her outfit. With a single tilt of his head, the man let her know that he'd picked her, and she waited for him to arrive at her side. The girls nearby twittered in hopes that he was coming for one of them.

"I'd let him into my nodbox," one murmured.

A nodbox was a bedroom, and Clara agreed. She'd definitely let this man crease her sheets. But as the women giggled with delight, she wanted to tell them not to concern themselves with their nerves. The man didn't have eyes for either one.

He was on his way to Clara.

She felt a rush of nervous excitement that started between her legs and flooded outward. It was rare for her to feel so self-conscious. She had a quality to her moves that came from within, a radiance on the floor that couldn't be taught. This man had it, too. That's what she'd been drawn to. Dancing could be a form of foreplay. But at most of these swing sessions, there simply hadn't been anyone she wanted to take to bed.

As a new song began, Lilly Faye and her Fire-Spittin' Fellas jumping into the groove, the man reached her side. He didn't say a word, simply put one hand on her waist and steered her onto the floor. This time, she wouldn't be passed onto someone new. She and her lindy shark would be partnered for the entire song. Knowing this, she took her time checking him out. Up close, he was even more attractive. Those dark, liquid eyes, like a silent film star's, were infinitely expressive. A deep, inky blue, they shined beneath the crystal chandelier. His hands were large, and firm, and they manoeuvred her through the moves with expertise, but didn't roam where they didn't belong. That was a surprise. Often men took the opportunity to fondle a partner, something Clara generally found distasteful. Now, she realised, she wouldn't have minded if his hands had wandered down a bit, if he'd tried a little stroking as they glided together.

Clara usually didn't have to think while she danced. Her feet easily followed her partner's lead. But this man was making her work for it. Executing several difficult steps from the very beginning, forcing her to concentrate. She forgot about what she hoped he might do and focused on making sure she was in step with him.

Other dancers spread out to give them some room, as if they sensed that something big was about to happen. And it was. As the first song blended into a second, and a third, the duo found their zone. When her partner flipped her into the air, she let out a little happy squeal, something totally unlike her. For the first time, the man smiled. It was as if a marble sculpture had cracked. For the rest of the dance, there was an ease between them. The moves came naturally. Clara no longer had to second-guess him, to think about where he was going. Instinctively, she followed.

When the music stopped so that Lilly Faye and her Fellas could take a breather, Clara kept following him – down the hallway from the main ballroom and into a small, unisex bathroom. This wasn't something she'd normally have done, but if he could dance like that, just imagine how he might make love. He locked the door behind them.

They could hear the music drifting in from the ballroom – someone had put on a CD by Big Bad Voodoo Daddy, and it was loud. People headed out to the bar, and voices lifted as spirits flowed. Alcohol mixed with dancing could make people rowdy. Clara was relieved not to be out there with the throng trying to make small talk.

The man lifted her up; she kicked out her heels automatically, as if he was still dancing with her. He wasn't. He set her down on the edge of the blue-and-white tiled sink and cradled her chin in one hand. Face to face, he was even more beautiful. His full mouth, almost indecently full for a man, came closer. Kissed her. Shivers ran through her body; she closed her eyes and floated on his kiss, not noticing when his fingers moved to the front of her dress and undid the tiny pearl buttons, buttons it had taken her ten minutes to fasten. She remembered standing in her bedroom, looking at her reflection, wondering whether this man would be present tonight. Whether he would like what she was wearing.

Beneath the vintage dress she wore a modern underwire lace bra and matching panties in crimson silk. The man stroked her breasts through the bra before unfastening the clasp and letting the racy lingerie fall to the floor. When she opened her eyes, she could see their reflection in the mirror across the way. They appeared dream-like, a perfect match. This was how it was meant to be.

The man took off his hat and set it on the counter. Then he tilted his head and watched her as she slid out of her dress to stand before him in her ruffled panties, garters, hose, and heels. Although he didn't speak, he seemed to want her to leave the stockings on. Quickly, he turned her so that they faced the mirror above the sink. He lowered her underpants and waited for her to step out of them. She watched in the mirror as he undid his slacks and opened them. She could see a flash of his boxers, polka-dots that matched her own dress – another indication of how perfect they were together.

Clara felt him lean against her, felt the length of his cock pressed against the skin of her heart-shaped ass. The silk of his boxers brushed the backs of her thighs, and now she sighed at the sensation. It was at this moment that he gripped onto her waist, letting her feel how ready he was. His cock was large and hard, and it moved forward, knowing its destination. Without a word, the man slipped it between her thighs, probing the wetness that awaited him. She'd gotten excited during their dancing, and the slick lubrication made it easy for him to part the lips of her pussy and slip inside. Just the head. Just a taste.

The sounds of the band started up in the other room, and to the lindy beat, he began to fuck her. Clara felt as if they were still dancing. Making love to him was as intricate as when he'd flipped her in the air, twirled her around him. Her heart raced with each stroke of his cock inside her, and she felt as if he were opening her up. Both to his throbbing sex, and to the music that swirled around them.

The bathroom's art deco style created a fantasy-like atmosphere, with its blue-tone of the mirror and tiled walls that echoed her sighs. Although he remained silent, the man seemed pleased by the way she moved, now rocking her body back and forth, helping him to reach the finish. He locked eyes with her in the mirror, and for the second time in the evening, he smiled. It began at the corners of his lips and moved up sparkle in his eyes. An intense connection flowed hot between them; she had been right to wait for him. She felt a sense of destiny as he slid his hands up her bare arms, stroking her skin, sending a fresh wave of tremors through her body.

She liked the silence, their lack of words. Some boys talked through the whole thing, and that ruined the effect. Lovemaking, Clara felt, shouldn't be full of chitchat. She craved mystery, magic – and with him, she had it. She felt that way about dancing. Some men wanted to talk instead of lindy. If you danced correctly, you could have a whole conversation without opening your mouth.

This man seemed to know that. He understood. Not saying a word as he filled her with his cock, held her gaze with his expression, now tricking his fingers along her breasts, pinching her nipples between his thumb and forefinger to make her moan and arch her body against his.

Oh, yes, that was the way to do it. To the sounds of the music, in the twinkling light of the small room, she strived to reach climax in synchronicity with him. She wanted the ride to feel as good for him as he was making it feel for her. She knew he must be growing more excited, but she couldn't tell from his face. Impishly, she squeezed him tight with her inner muscles, watching for his expression to change.

His eyes closed, long lashes dark against his pale skin, strong jaw set as he held her tight. Yes, it was going to happen. Now. She could sense it. And she closed her eyes, too, as those pulses of pleasure flooded through her, finally gripping onto the edge of the sink to hold herself steady.

The best part happened then. He didn't withdraw, remained inside her, and she could feel him growing hard again almost instantaneously. She sighed with pleasure as he extended the ride, this time taking her harder, faster. She felt as if she might literally dissolve with pleasure. All of the sensations were heightened, and when he brought one hand between her legs, plucking her clit with knowledgeable fingers, she came against his hand, biting her bottom lip hard to keep from actually screaming with pleasure. She felt weightless, as she had when he'd tossed her into the air. The thrill of it brought a flush to her cheeks, a sheen to her eyes. When she looked in the mirror, she seemed transformed.

They stayed locked together for several moments, and then he pulled out and tucked himself back into his suit. She expected him to look altered, as well. After

21

something as spectacular as that, shouldn't he appear changed? She was surprised to notice that he hardly looked rumpled at all, his shirt still cleanly pressed, the fine crease on his pants in place. But she felt suddenly exposed, with her bra and panties on the floor, her dress a puddle of polka-dotted fabric. It would take her a bit to sort herself out. He seemed to understand this, and he gave her a final kiss and a wink, then nodded with his head for her to fasten up her clothes.

He would meet her outside, she guessed, and she watched him leave, then hurried to lock the door behind him, her heart pounding so loudly, for a moment it sounded like the drum section from Lilly Faye's band. Her fingers trembled as she rebuttoned her dress, and it took her longer than it had earlier in the evening. Misbuttoning and starting again, desperate to finish so that she could get back out on the floor and dance with him again.

Back in the ballroom, as a new song began, she was certain he would hurry to her side, would lift her up in the air so that her dress twirled as it had been meant to. Her crimson ruffled panties would show, and the scent of sex would waft around her like perfume. From now on, they would be partnered together, showing off for the rest of the crowd. They would go back to her place that night, and in the morning she would take him to her favourite vintage store on Third Avenue. Would try on clothes for him. Would let him dress her. There were so many things they could do together –

But when she exited the rest room and saw him standing by the wall, he didn't seem to focus on her, his eyes roaming the crowd. She wanted to wave her hand up, to call out that she was right here, waiting. The two women who'd stood next to her before were now at the bar across the way, and Clara watched, dismayed, as the man turned in their direction. The girls were aware of his fixation, and one let out a high, flirtatious laugh that reached Clara even above the music. The man adjusted his suspenders in a practised, casual move, then fixed his hat so that it tilted rakishly forward.

The room blurred in Clara's vision, as she realised that like a shark, he was moving again through the water of the dancers. After another kill.

Blue Sky Sideways

From my position on the bed, I can see the window, partially opened to let in the late afternoon light, and the wall, striped with lines of colour from the shades. I'm on my stomach, with my wrists securely cuffed and fastened over my head to a hook in the wall. My legs are spread apart and ankles bound to the bedposts of my Mistress' queen-sized canopy. She's not in the house. She tied me here and told me her plans for the evening. And then she left.

Now that she's gone, I wish she'd blindfolded me. Now that I'm alone, I realise that what I thought was a kindness is really another form of punishment. Deprivation of sight can be comforting. This is hell – able to see only a bit of the window, a bit of the fading light. I can turn my head the other way, though the movement is uncomfortable, but all there is to see on that side is a terrifying reflection of me in a wall-sized mirror. A confrontation I am not at this moment ready or willing to meet. How freaky, to look into my own eyes, to see the pain there. Or, more honestly, the desire for pain. Can't exactly describe it to you, if you don't already know. If you're not one of the cult who either revel in giving pain or relish receiving it.

I'm of the latter crew, and I dream of my Mistress'

tortures. The feel of her cold hands as she fastens the bindings in place. The movement, subtle, gentle, as she slips the blindfold over my eyes and ties it beneath my hair. I come thinking of her teeth finding purchase on one of the rings that adorns my nipples, my labia, and pulling, tearing at my flesh. I get the most joy when she makes me scream.

Hard to explain it to a novice. To one of the as-yet uninitiated. But I've got the time, if you've got the inclination to listen. My Mistress won't be back for hours, and I can whisper to you until then. After that, I'd advise you to hide in the closet and stay very still. If she catches you here, you'll be in for the same treatment that awaits me. And for a novice, for one as pure as yourself, that might be a bit extreme.

So, meant to ask you, but somehow got confused, are you one of us? Are you a dark horse that rides the fringe of society? Does the thought of a thin black collar around your pale throat make you wet? When you were pierced for the first time, did just the brush of your blouse against your nipples make you come?

That's how it was for me. I've always loved secrets, refuse to give myself up entirely for anyone, and the secret piercings were my first dance with darkness. I remember the smell of the place – the Gauntlet – the near-angelic smile of the black-haired demon as he cleaned me with alcohol before readying the needle. Addictive, it was, the rush of the pain. Not long enough. Over much too quickly. But my Mistress knew what I was thinking and she assured me that we would be back. And soon.

That's how it was for me. The desire to please her. And my pain pleases her. My pain makes me beautiful to her. My ugliness, the tears that mar my finely-cut features, the furrows that line my brow as I fight back the screams – these are the things that my Mistress loves best.

"Look at yourself," she hisses, grabbing fistfuls of my black hair, shiny as a colt's, and pulling me upright. "Look into the mirror and tell me what you see."

I close my eyes against this request. I don't want to see the reflection, the evil twin lurking beneath a frozen screen of mercury. I don't want to know the part of me that stares so calmly back through the glass.

The palm of her open hand slaps my cheek, bringing the welcome pain to my soul that makes it easier for me to obey her. I wish sometimes that I could obey her without the need to be punished. I've told her as much, but she just bares her teeth at me in the grimace that passes for one of her smiles, bares her teeth and strokes my hair and croons, lullaby-style, "Darling, if you didn't need pain, you wouldn't be my slave. I do so love to make you cry."

Staring at my reflection in the mirror, the tears that slide down my cheeks, the puffy hurt look to my lips – it's like staring at a stranger. And then her hand on my face again, slapping the other side this time, bringing a fresh rosy blush to my cheek, just to even me out. Watching that is like watching the start of a fire. The spark, the glow, before the raging blaze. Watching that is like buying a ticket to hell.

"What do you see?" she asks, biting off the words that could follow: "What do you see, cunt?" she could say. "What do you see, slave?", "What do you see, whore?"

I see a need, burning, engulfing. I see a yearning. A desire that only my Mistress can meet. She fills me. She holds me. She bends me until my will is broken. She scatters the pieces so far apart that I can never be whole again. How I long to submit to her.

How I long to please her.

"You see a sinful little fuck," she tells me, slapping me again as she lists the correct answers, not A, B, or C, but all of the above. "You see an evil soul. You see a sinner."

Yes. All of those things, Mistress. All of those things and more.

When we met, at a club in the Village, a dark hole that suited my needs perfectly, she slipped up behind me, wrapped one arm around my waist pulling me back against her, and she hissed, "I will break you."

Oh God. If you are a novice, I can't explain it to you. If you're normal – if you don't need pain (to give or receive it) then you won't understand. Then you'll think I'm a sick, perverted creature – which I am – and you'll leave the room, quietly closing the door behind you. That's fine. Go, if you need to. Go, if you can't take it.

I'll wait here by myself for her.

I'll wait here, with my wrists cuffed too tightly together, my legs pulled to their widest point possible, stretched until I feel that ache in every muscle, and I'll wait. Until my Mistress comes home and pulls her cane from the stand. I'll wait for her to position herself by the bed and use that thin bamboo cane to stripe me from my shoulder blades to the soles of my feet. I'll wait patiently for her to do everything she promised before she left – "I'm gonna mark you tonight. I'm gonna make you mine. I'm gonna break you."

Do you get it? If you're still here, then you must get it. You must be kin, a blood sister, to understand the waves of white-hot need that ride through me at all times. Place your hand against your throat and feel the lifeline of your blood pulsing there. C'mon, press a little harder now, I want it to be a struggle for you to breathe over the pressure. It's not scary, child. You're doing this to yourself. You have all the power. Honest. You can stop any time you want.

Next test. Take your blouse off, or at least unbutton the top three or four buttons. Nice little bra you've got on there. Black. I like it. My Mistress would like it. She thinks black bras are very sexy, especially when worn under good girl clothes. I try to please her, I try to wear what she likes. But sometimes I forget. I'm glad you didn't forget, this being your first time with her. It's important that you show her your respect.

Okay, now, I want you to pinch your right nipple between your thumb and your finger. Harder. I'll tell you when you can stop. I want you to feel this, and I want you to think of your Mistress doing this to you. She'll pinch your nipples until they go numb. She'll clip clothespins on them. She'll use those nasty clamps with the ridges and the chain between them that will humiliate you by jingling every time you walk. But for now, you're to show your obedience by pinching them yourself.

Good girl.

Describe the sensation to me. C'mon. Just because I'm tied here, doesn't mean I don't have power. I do, child. I can stop talking to you. I can stop spinning my tales for you. And I know you wouldn't like that. I can tell by the way you're looking at me, the haunted look in your eyes. The desire. It comes off you in waves, my darling, like perfume, the sweetest scent. And mingled with it is the smell of fear. That's good, very good. You should be afraid.

Okay, now. Pinch the other. Harder this time. I want your nipples to be throbbing with heat and fire. I want you to bite down on your bottom lip to stifle the cry. That hurts more than you thought it would, doesn't it? But as soon as you release, the feeling is replaced, right? By something entirely different. A flood of sensations, sort of swollen, but tingling. It feels different, doesn't it, child? It feels… good.

Oh, yessss. Come closer to me. Sit yourself down right on the edge of the bed. I want you to look in the mirror, girl. I want you to stare at yourself while you take your blouse all the way off. Just throw it on the ground. Now your bra. Now pinch those nipples again. Both at the same time. Keep holding. I'll tell you when you can stop. Don't look down, girl. Stare right into your eyes while you're doing it. And tell me, tell me….

What do you see?

You see a naughty girl, don't you? You see a slut, a whore, someone who deserves to be punished. Of course you do. I can read it in your eyes. Even if you thought you were a Mistress. Even if you thought you were the one who'd be in charge. You're not in charge now, are you? You're not telling ME what to do, are you? See how easy that is? That switch of power. The slide, the shift, the subtle dance. Ahh, child, it doesn't matter that my limbs are fastened to this bed. Power is not in the body. It's in the mind.

(You can let go now. Mmmm, I wish I could put my tongue on those beauties and cool you down.)

Confused, aren't you? Don't worry. You're supposed to be. All I'm doing is giving you what you want. What you need. More than that. Darker than that. Deeper than that. Older than that. I'm giving you what you deserve.

You've known for a long time. I can tell. You've tripped with your naughty fantasies, slid your fingers under the sheets at night to find that throbbing little jewel between your thighs. Pressing, rolling, tickling it between your fingertips, you've thought of the most sinful desires. You've given in to them. Understand this, then, child. Understand that your chums, your mates, your gang – many of them would be disgusted if you told them what you want. They're thinking sweet thoughts. Happy thoughts. They're thinking of kd lang on a Harley zooming up to them at the prom and whisking them off into the sunset. And that's just naughty enough for their pure minds. A Harley, they're thinking. Ooooh. Bad.

But not you, slut. You're thinking of bending over the desk at school, having the professor bare your ass while she whips those tender thighs of yours with her thick leather belt. Gets worse, doesn't it? The whole class is watching, aren't they? All those eyes on you, watching as the edge of your skirt is pulled up and tucked into the waistband, as your panties are yanked down your thighs and left to hang (left to humiliate you) down around your ankles. The whole class is watching as she reaches for a cane from the stand by the door, reaches for it and shows it to you before bringing it down on your bare haunches.

What does she want you to do, girl? Tell me. It's your fantasy.

Does she want you to kiss it before she punishes you with it? Does she want to let those first teardrops (caused solely by fear) to rain on the bamboo before the weapon marks your pale skin? What does she want you to do?

Does she want you to come? Is that what it's about? Would you come in front of your peers? Would you let them see you writhe in combination of pain and pleasure? Is that what you want, girl? Is that what it takes?

You think of them moving closer, of their hands on you, inspecting you, touching the welts as they bloom against your pale skin. Stroking the marks that she leaves – reminder marks. Poor thing. You want to feel them touch you. I can tell.

Ah, you're a bad girl. I knew you were. I can usually tell. Don't you love that, my darling? Don't you come to that image at night, those naughty fingers of yours moving in those tingling circles, 'round and 'round your pulsing clit?

You come to it, late at night, when everyone else in your house is asleep – wouldn't want to wake them with the sound of your bed shaking, would you? It's okay. I'll ease your troubled mind for you. It's okay to think the things you do, to want the things you do. It's even okay to do them... just look at me, tied so tightly to the bed that it's hard for me to move, thinking only of what my Mistress will do to me when she returns. Especially when she learns that I've been talking to you. I was supposed to be spending the afternoon contemplating my sins, my transgressions. You know that it's the anticipation that always makes the moment. It builds inside until you can't contain it. Until it's too strong. Too wild. Until it's screaming inside to get out.

And she'll be angry with me for wasting time talking with you. No, don't worry. I'm sure you wouldn't rat on me. But I will. I'll confess as soon as she walks through the door. I'll say, "Mistress Jane, I have something to tell you." For your sake, my darling, I hope that you're gone. Because she will want to take care of us both at the same time. So unless you're truly secure in your desire for pain, I'd recommend that you either hide or vanish.

What would she do? C'mon, cutie, do you really have to ask? No. I know you don't. I know that you just want to hear me say the words. It's much more real when someone else says the words, isn't it? When someone else says, "Lower your panties, child, and bend over my lap. You're gonna get a spanking." Mmm. I caught the look in your eyes when I said that. Has it really been that long, darling? Have you never scrambled over the lap of a displeased lover and felt her fingertips sliding beneath your underpants and pulling them down your legs? Poor thing. What you've been missing.

But I was telling you a story, wasn't I? I was telling you about Jane, about the night we met. It was one of those bizarre circumstances. I'd decided that I didn't need anyone. I was tired of looking, tired of the quest to find a decent Mistress who wasn't completely psycho. In fact, I'd just plain given up, and I was taking myself out for a pre-slumber drink at the club down the street from my apartment. It always happens like that – love, I mean – when you don't need it, when you are totally secure with who you are and what you're doing, that's when it hits you.

Literally, in my case.

Jane came up to the bar in her panther-stride, silently stalking behind me and appearing at my right in with a magician's ease. Now you see her, now you don't. She lit a cigarette and then, without saying a word, slipped it between my lips. I will never forget that feeling, her fingers pressed to the pucker of my mouth as she held the fag there for me to inhale. I did, took a nice long drag, and then stared at her as she brought the fag to her own mouth and inhaled.

We still hadn't said a word to each other. She hadn't even asked me if I smoked. She'd just assumed. (In fact, I'd given up the cancer-sticks six months before, but the taste was just as nasty and sweet as I'd remembered, and it stirred a longing within me that wasn't only for the nicotine.) Eyes still holding mine, she leaned forward again, but this time she didn't pass over the cigarette. This time she moved in closer and kissed me. Softly.

Gently. Her lips brushing over mine like a silken handkerchief, like the coloured ones I'd worn in my back pocket years before to let people know that, yes, I liked Victorian games and corsetry (white lace) and, yes, I would be tied down if so desired by lover (grey), and, yes, I would be whipped (black).

"Jane," she said as she pulled away, exhaling the smoke that still lingered in her lungs. My hand went out and caught hers, "Rice," I said.

"Last name?"

Shake of my golden curls. "Nickname."

She left it at that. We weren't after small talk, neither of us.

"You done here?"

I waited a beat, staring into her eyes again, watching the colours within them shift and change in the dim light. She had chameleon eyes, now green, now blue, now grey. They stayed on this last colour, going a dull metal hue as I watched, and then, deep within them, I saw the spirals of black. Vein-like, the way white marble is veined, the way the sidewalks crack after an earthquake. Swirls of black against grey, they cracked further, swallowing me up, promising me, promising me…

"Yeah, I'm done."

Her grip was iron-strong, firm around my waist, shuffling me out of the pub and down the block in a rapid, military step. No words again. Energy moving between us instead. I trusted her and I let her set the beat.

She lived in a Brownstone then, up three flights of rickety wooden stairs, and she led me through her entrance and to the bedroom without a single hostess-like word of welcome. No, "Here's my living room" nonsense. No "Would you like another drink?" stall for time. Her hands were on me, all over me, leading, pushing, prodding me down the dark hall to her room, a quick heave and onto the bed. And then she stood a few steps back, her breathing hastened, and stared at me.

I wondered what she was seeing. Thin, college-type. Faded jeans, black velvet turtleneck. Blonde hair in ringlets, gone platinum from too many days at the beach. Pale blue eyes, darker lashes than a blonde should own, wild lips still stained with berry-gloss.

I wondered if she could see beyond that. No fear. No fear. No fear. I have nothing left to lose. Take me. Use me. Break/abuse me. Sinful twisted fantasies are here for you to find. Cheap, free for the asking, no cover charge…

"Lie down. On your back."

Done. I closed my eyes to avoid staring at the nothingness of her ceiling.

"Lift your hips."

Her hands were on the waistband, unzipping my jeans, pulling them down to my ankles, leaving them there, caught in place by my patent leather boots. My panties came down next, caught to the same place, a bit of white cotton that felt soft against my ankles.

"Would you prefer to be tied?"

Shake of my head, not bothering to move the curls away once they'd partially covered my face. I could feel the blush to my cheeks, but I didn't want to call attention to it. I didn't know what was driving her at this point, what I might inadvertently do to stop her, to anger her. I forced myself to be as still and as non-combatant as I could, hoping with all my soul that this wasn't a dream. A tease. A night-time fantasy.

She was at my side on the bed, parting the lips of my pussy with both thumbs, opening me up and observing me there, the colours, the gradations of pinks, dark rose to pale petal. I could smell my scent already, and she could, too. This made her laugh, as did the gloss that came away on her fingertips when she removed her hands.

"You were wet in the bar."

A statement. I didn't know if she expected or required an answer.

"You were."

"Yes…"

"That's how I found you. I smelled you from across the room."

The flush to my cheeks grew darker, creeping along the line of my jaw and to my neck. I could feel the heat of embarrassment there, but also a new flood of honey that coated my thighs. Her voice was turning me on.

"You've been alone for a long time, haven't you?"

"Yes…"

"Long enough to have forgotten how to respond to one in charge."

There, stated easily for me to interpret. I now knew our game. ("But hold on," a tiny voice said inside me, "This doesn't feel like a game. Not like the kinds you're used to. This feels dangerous. And real.")

"Oh." Out of my mouth before I could stop it, a sigh, dark with need, hungry with want. "Yes…" still unfinished, wishing I knew the correct answer, not caring about the consolation prize, I was going for what was behind door number three. "It has been a long time, Mistress."

Dark chuckle that didn't let me know whether I'd won the new car or whether I was about to join the ranks of the runners up.

"That's better. Not perfect, but better."

This is not a game, I thought again. It's not a game with a capital M for her and a lower-case s for me. Thank

God, thank you God, I've waited much too long for this. Waited my whole life for this. Deep within myself, I was still sane enough to wonder whether it was truly God I should be thanking. If He is the creator of all, than he created me, with my multitude of sinful passions, wicked thoughts, harmful desires. But it just doesn't seem right.

She interrupted my thoughts with a blindfold, brought tight over my eyes and then slipped expertly behind my neck. I lifted up for her to make it easier for her to tie it. My eyes were closed beneath the smooth material, and in that new place there was no light.

"You don't need to be tied," she repeated to me. "But I will tie you. In the future, whenever I want to, I will tie you. For now, I'd like to see how much you can take. This is for your own sake, so I know where our starting ground is. What I have to work with. How far you want to go." A pause, "Though, you really must understand that it's not about your wants, your desires. It's about needs. Yours and mine. And I will take you beyond the edge of your world. I will take you into mine."

Then silence. And darkness. And I lay there waiting for it to begin. It takes some courage, you know, to wait like that, without screaming, without begging. The pain is always better than the moments before. Better because you're already immersed. It's like dipping your toes into icy water – oh, how awful – always much better to be thoroughly drenched, that heart-stopping feeling of the icy waves surrounding you.

In horror movies it's described as the monster behind the closed door. Your mind will always create a much more frightening monster than any F/X technician ever could. Why? Because you are the sole owner of your own fears. You have named each one, created each one. Once the door opens to reveal an actor in a silly costume, the fear is over. But those few precious moments before… those are worth cherishing.

As I cherish these… tied here and waiting for my Mistress' return. Yes, I still refer to her as such. But only when discussing our relationship. At the times that she beats me, she is nameless. At the times that she takes me higher, she is all things. And nothing. And I am the same.

I have no religion to get in the way of my worshiping her. Or, better yet, I have a religion that is of my own creation. I have a religion and she is my god. Does that surprise you? Does that make you quiver, make you want to stand out of the way to see if some lightning bolt will fell me? Don't worry, kiddo. Nothing can hurt me. I am already in hell.

What are you looking at now? The chest by the door? That's where she keeps her toys, her props, the tricks of the trade. Go ahead, open it up. It's not Pandora's box, sweetheart. Nothing will fly out and scare you. Just open it up and poke around, see if you recognise anything. See if you like anything. I'll tell you my favourites as you reach them. There are some sweet toys there, some vibrators, pure pleasure enhancers. And some items of sole discipline.

You stopped when I said that word. Do you like it? Does it do something to you inside. Yesss, it does. I can tell. Oh, you are one of us, little one. And let me give you another reading – free, of course, I'm not like one of those wacky psychic member hot lines – this reading is of your future. And I see you in a lot of pain. Yes, just as I thought. Come here and look at your face in the mirror. Your eyes went down as I said that, your lashes fluttered and your cheeks grew hot. You want pain, don't you, darling? You crave it. You yearn for it. You deserve it.

Don't tremble like that, sweetheart. It's okay. I wish

my hands were free so I could hold you. As it is, you'll have to snuggle up against me if you want comfort. That's it. That's the girl. Come lay by my side and whisper your fantasies to me. You can't say anything that would offend me. I'm much too far gone for that.

There, doesn't that feel better? Tell me, sweetheart. Tell me everything… tell me everything that you want.

No? Cat got your tongue? That's all right, too. Settle down against me, get comfortable, and listen to my voice. I will tell you stories…

Hangover Tuesday

Monday. The trail was as cold as the rain pouring down, as cold as my ex-girlfriend's grey eyes when she'd told me goodbye for the final time. I knew exactly what it would take to make me feel better. A hot body, a warm bed, and a night of no sleep. Instead, I forced myself to settle for a quick cup of coffee in a dingy cafe. At least, it was a place out of the rain. And maybe, if luck was on my side, I'd be able to gather a bit of information. You never can tell who knows what these days.

Especially in Amsterdam.

The handsome blond creature behind the counter poured me a brimming cup of thick black stuff that looked like mud and tasted only a little bit worse. As I choked down my first swallow, he offered over the menu. I'm accustomed to Norm's, the L.A. diner on the corner of La Brea and Vine, where the coffee is bad, the service is worse, and none of the waiting staff remotely resemble Greek gods. So it took me a moment to realise that what I was perusing was a list of ten types of marijuana.

"Ten of the *best* types," the blond Adonis explained, as if reading my mind. "In order of my favourites from top to bottom."

"What's the difference?" I asked. Sure, I'd tried weed before. Smoked myself silly once with Sandrine. We'd spent the afternoon like kittens on catnip, rolling around in our queen-sized bed, nipping at each other. Biting. Pretending that we didn't have claws. I knew what marijuana could do to me. But unlike single malt, which I can discern down to the type of barrel it's been blended in, I am no reefer connoisseur.

"See for yourself," the boy teased, pushing a pre-rolled joint to me and offering up the flame of his battered, silver lighter.

As I said, the lead I'd been following had all but vanished. Disappeared into one of the winding canals that encircle this magical city. There wasn't anything to keep me from picking up the joint and taking a puff. Nothing, but my conscience.

Could I get blasted on my employer's dime?

That took me less than a second to think about. What does a dime buy these days, anyway? Not even a phone call. As I inhaled the fragrant smoke, the counter cutie leaned forward, waiting. On the exhale, he locked his mouth to mine and drew in my breath. His lips were soft, and they knew a thing or four about kissing. Inside, he left me all flustered, my stomach free-falling to my knees, my nether regions doing a perfectly passable impression of a flash flood. But a good private dick can keep her cool, no matter what the situation.

"Is that service included in the price of the joint?" I asked playing coy before taking another hit.

"I've got a thing for Americans," he confessed in his accentless English. "You all do something to me."

"It can't be Americans," I disagreed. "It must be the pot." As I spoke, I started to feel the high creep through my body. For some reason, this buzz was beginning at my extremities and working inward, an exhilarating sensation that made me feel suddenly invincible. I took another drag and held the smoke in deep, letting it cloud up my lungs like the dirt-coloured smog that hangs low over Pasadena.

"Americans," I continued in earnest, "are nothing special."

He said I was wrong. And he said he could prove it.

Who was I to challenge him? I couldn't even feel my head any more, much less make a serious argument. The boy told me his name, which I promptly forgot in a fit of giggles, and then he helped me to his apartment, happily situated right upstairs.

What happened next, I'm embarrassed to relate. Not because it wasn't good, but because I was still on the clock. But the boy wasn't the one paying my way, wasn't paying to play, he was simply fulfilling my fantasies. A hot body. A warm bed. And a night of no sleep.

It went something like this….

The apartment was practically empty. There was a mouldy-looking green sofa slumped along one wall, a pull-down bed that looked as if it had never been put back up, and a view so breathtaking that I had to stand pressed against the windowpane and stare outside, trying to soak up the beauty with the palms of my hands. The lights of nearby buildings reflected eerily in the slick-surfaced water of the canal, making me remember Sandrine, once again. She would have liked that scene, and I wondered where she was, what she was doing, and who she was doing it with.

Then the boy, the sweet, sweet boy, was at my side, helping me to forget.

He said, "Stoned sex is something special."

And I said, "ssssss" because all of his words started with the letter s.

He undressed me while I stood at the window, and I

knew his hands were on my body only because I could see them when I looked down. Everything felt surreal, as if I'd entered one of Salvador Dali's melting prints. My clothes melted away. My hesitance melted away. And suddenly there was just me and him, doing that dirty dance they don't teach you in school. His parts interlocked with mine, as the two of us became one.

And then the one of us became three.

I didn't understand it at first. As the high slowly wore away, I could feel him, his strong, taut body against mine, his hands roaming up and down, carelessly teasing my nipples, stroking the hollow of my neck. Then, as I watched, a second set of hands joined the first. Female hands, long red-lacquered nails, silky skin. Hands I'd held a million times before. Fingers that had pinched my clit until it felt as if it would burst.

I shook my head hard, to clear the vision, but sometimes that doesn't help. Sometimes that only serves to confuse things even more. This was one of those times. Suddenly, the delicate female hands were removed, and when I turned, there she was, leaning against the wall.

Not such a bad detective, I thought to myself. Pride, as usual, my initial emotion. I had stumbled upon her even when there were no more clues. I had followed her scent, my favourite of all worldly smells, and even masked by the fragrant marijuana perfume, I'd found her.

Sandrine.

"I missed you," I said stupidly, before her fingers reached my lips and quieted them with a single touch. I understood. She didn't want to talk. She wanted to do. Fine by me. Actions resonate louder than words. They last longer. They mean more.

The boy was with us still, and he managed to

accentuate the positive. His being there helped. Helped join us, blend us, until there we were again, one beast made of three. And for a moment, it was sublime. It was perfection.

Unfortunately, I'm not a perfect being, I needed more. Was this why Sandrine left me in the first place? Have I always needed something else? I don't know. I only know that I reached for it, my eyes pleading, and after a moment she gave in.

On second inspection, the apartment was less empty than I'd thought. Maybe I'm not such a good dick, after all. Displayed on a counter by the bed were the types of toys you see for sale in every sultry sex shop on the canals. Dildos and handcuffs. Blindfolds and paddles. Shiny vinyl outfits that are so pretty when they get wet, no matter what type of liquid glosses their surface. Use your imagination.

Sandrine reached for her favourite type of weapon, a device that looked as if it had been specifically crafted to fit her hand. The crop had a braided tip and a bone handle. From the first sight of it, a dangerous rush screamed through me. I knew the pain it could inflict. Knew how much I could take, and knew that she would push me further. Punish me for the very need that flamed within my soul.

But not this time.

She said the boy's name and he turned to look at her. Glazed green eyes. Chiselled cheeks. A picture torn from a magazine. On the surface, he had everything anyone could ever want. But as I stared at him, I understood that he was like me. He needed more inside. And while I watched, she gave it to him. Gave what was rightfully mine, rightfully deserved by me, to him.

On the bed, on his stomach, his back all beautiful lines

of muscles and sinews. Strong thighs. Fine ass. His golden skin an unmarred canvas. She offered cuffs, but he refused. Offered a blindfold, a gag. He wanted none. He only wanted me…to hold his hands. Sighing, I took my place at the head of the bed and did as he requested.

Sandrine barely looked at him as she worked. She locked eyes with me and let me know that each stroke against his fair flesh was mine. She burned me with her look while giving him what I wanted.

"Count," she said, and he did. Entirely still, steeling himself for each blow, he counted the strokes for her. His voice was low, a level over a whisper, and the only thing that gave away his pain was how tightly he held my hands. Squeezed them until the tips of my fingers became purple-hued and numb, but I didn't try to get free.

"That's right," she hissed at him. Or hissed at me. I wasn't sure. "That's what you need. What you deserve."

She took him to the edge of his limits without even breaking a sweat on her radiant brow. Then she took him past, to that most secret place where boundaries are broken and fantasies come true. She didn't stop until she'd painted a new picture on his skin, a picture made of flesh and blood. Didn't stop until he arched his body and came violently against the mattress in a series of silent shudders, the tears finally bursting free and sliding down his sculptured face. But I knew him as I know myself, and I knew that it wasn't the pain that made him cry.

It was the pleasure.

Then there was silence, his fingers slipping out of my grasp, his body curving into a foetal position on the mattress, finding solace in silence as sleep took him away.

We watched him for a long time, Sandrine and I. She sat

on one side of the bed; I sat on the other. There was heat between us, and I could guess what was coming, but I didn't rush it. I wanted to ask her too many questions. Who the boy was. What he meant to her. What their connection was. Yet I understood that it didn't really matter. He was a second-string player in this performance of ours, a tool, someone to dally with when nobody else was around.

"Who's looking for me?" Sandrine finally whispered over the boy's still body.

I turned to stare at her, stunned. Didn't she get it?

"You're following me. You tracked me here. I have sources in the city. I know you walked down every winding street, looked in every window, asked questions to anyone who would listen. You're hot on the trail. And someone's paying." She paused a beat. "Somebody always pays."

She was right. I had strolled down the alleys where the girls are for sale. Stopped at the windows and watched the shows. Went to every dive bar and pulled her picture from my pocket. But she was slow. She didn't realise the truth. Gracefully, I threw her a single clue.

"You know I never reveal that type of information," I said, and a smile lit my face against my will.

She waited, silent, that bone-handled crop now resting against her thigh. I bit my lip as I looked at it. If I confessed, would she give me what she gave him? Or did she already know. Did she just want to hear me say it aloud?

"You didn't come all this way just for me –" she started, but then she looked in my eyes, and for the first time, she understood.

I had hired myself to find her. That's why it was so easy for me to take advantage of this particular idiot of a client. It was, in fact, my dime I was spending, my own time I was fucking away.

"Oh, baby," she said, and I could tell from her expression that we were getting close to the end of the line. That hers was the very next stop. "I'm sorry." She meant those words, I could tell, and then her fist closed around the handle of the crop and she made it better. For just a short time, she made everything all right.

I must confess, I lied before. A hot body, warm bed, night of no sleep…sounds plenty poetic, but it's just not for me. Night or day, it doesn't matter. What I need is a dominant hand and an unforgiving soul, and most importantly, I need Sandrine.

The boy had undressed me. All she had to do was stretch me out to my limits, in front of that view I'd so admired. My hands above my head, cuffed because she said I'd need it. Cuffed and suspended from the bar over the window. My legs kicked out wide, opening my hips, spreading my cunt, offering everything to her, to use as she pleased.

And what pleased her was hurting me. Which was fine, because that's what pleased me, as well. She used the crop as if it were an extension of herself. I felt her strength behind every stroke, felt her mark me with it, my eyes open and staring at the canal, at the fairy lights that glittered in the dark water. I knew the boy was awake, and that he was listening, but he seemed to understand that this dance had nothing to do with him. Yet feeling his eyes on me only added to my pleasure.

I had an audience. That made it more real.

She gave me breaks when I needed them, letting me sip from her pocket flask. The type of single malt that I learned to like because it was always her drink of choice. The alcohol burned, but it was nothing compared to the pain she inflicted. Berry-coloured welts that would stand out against my pale skin long after she'd left me again.

The pain kept me in the present. It helped me to focus, and just like the boy, I didn't cry. Sandrine rewarded me for that. When she was finished, when I could feel the air kissing the places where she'd broken the skin, she granted me a final prize. Bent on her knees in front of me, she peeled open my nether lips, slid her tongue inside me to fix what was broken. Her fingertips ran up and down my bruised skin, her tongue made dreamy, creamy circles around my clit. The pain and pleasure wove itself together until I didn't know which was which. But that was the whole point, wasn't it?

We'd been together long enough for her to know what I like. We'd been apart long enough for every touch of her tongue inside me to set my nerve endings on fire. She worked me carefully, knowing exactly what she was doing every step of the way. I tried hard to get free when I came. I wanted to cradle her face, to stroke her hair. The cuffs let me do neither, which was exactly the way Sandrine wanted it. And as the vibrations slammed through me, I suddenly realised that she was right. Somebody always pays. This time, I understood that the somebody had been me.

When I woke in the morning, I was alone in the bed. The room was empty, the curtains drawn. But what could I expect? After all, it was Tuesday. Hangover Tuesday. And I was back on the trail of a beautiful woman whose cold, grey eyes had told me goodbye without needing any assistance from her lips.

Andrew And The Blade

I met Andrew at a bar near Stanford. I was reading a book by Jeanette Winterson and Andrew and his buddy wouldn't leave me alone. They said they'd never seen a girl read at a bar before. Few people have. For some reason, after working alone all day, I find it calming to be in loud, raucous arenas. And in these places, I can tune out the world around me, like white noise, and relax.

Andrew pushed up against me, offering to buy me a drink, taking the book out of my hands and reading the title: *Sexing the Cherry*. It's not about what he thought it was about, but he had fun kidding me, seeing the blush that comes naturally to my cheeks. I'm fair-skinned. Blushes show up on me like splashes of iridescent, crimson paint.

More out of boredom than anything else, I ended up going home with him. I hadn't been with a guy for a long time. We fucked in his water bed, a first for me. There was a neon "open" sign above his bed, and the light gilded our skin in a pale blue, reminding me of corpses, of the light in some after hours clubs, an unhealthy, unearthly glow.

Afterwards, with a sheen of sweat on our bodies, he lit a cigarette and started talking. It was the type of getting to know you chit-chat most people do *before* they fuck. I didn't engage. I tuned him out, something I'm very good at. As he spoke, blowing silvery smoke rings at his ceiling, his stories grew wilder. I watched the sheets and saw he was arousing himself. I started paying more attention.

"I'm seeing this girl," he said, meaning that he used to date her, not that they were currently involved. "She was into all sorts of crazy things. Handcuffs. Rope. Blindfolding."

"You or her?" I asked, startling him since I'd been quiet for so long.

"What?"

"Who was blindfolded?"

He took a long drag of his cigarette, then said, "Me."

I smiled. I was liking this girl already.

"So she blindfolded me this one night and asked if she could tie me to the bed."

I looked at Andrew. He's at least 225lb, over six feet tall. A big bear of a guy. His chest is covered in thick black fur. His blue eyes are light and clear. He's muscular, with a bit of a gut. The photograph on his refrigerator shows him in top form, and when he's at his peak, he's gorgeous. Even a little heavy, he's attractive.

"How big is the girl?" I ask.

"Little, like you."

"So, no threat?"

He shakes his head and lights another cigarette. "But I've never been tied down before. I don't know how I'm going to like it."

"It's a lark," I say, shrugging.

He nods. "Yeah. I'm thinking, try it once. If I hate it I can break out of it." He blows smoke rings some more. "She knows how to do the knots, though. She really ties me down. Then she starts rubbing different things on me."

"Oils?"

"No, like objects. She wants me to guess the name of each thing she touches me with."

"Touches you –"

"You know." He sounds embarrassed. "My cock."

I nod. I know. It's sticking straight up, now that we're talking about it, and I reach over and stroke him through the sheet.

"She's got this furry thing, like a stuffed animal, and she starts with that. I know what it is, and I guess it after a moment. It feels sorta good against my balls, but she stops and does something else. This time it takes me longer."

I wait.

"It's a stocking she was wearing, and that feels good, too. Next, it's her bra, something really soft and nice. Then, it's something cold. The glass she was drinking from. I'm guessing them all. No problem."

I bend and start kissing his cock through the sheet. He's got satin sheets on the water bed. I like that. It's unexpected.

"She's touching me with all sorts of stuff. You know, a coaster. A CD. Cold things. Then something warm, a towel that had been near the heat duct. She's grabbing things willy-nilly from around the apartment. And my cock is like huge. It's bursting. Every time she brushes it with something soft, I'm about to spurt."

I'm using my open mouth now. I can taste his skin through the sheet.

"I tell her. I say, 'Carol. I'm gonna come. Any second now. Stop touching me with these things and climb aboard.' She says, 'One more, baby.' So, fine. One more."

His body grows totally still. I feel a change in him and look up.

"And it's cold. This last thing. It's cold against me. I don't wanna guess it. I say, 'I give up.' She says, 'I'll keep rubbing it on you until you guess.' I really… I mean, I just don't want to. 'Come on,' she says, like I'm chicken. 'Guess.' I can't think. It's cold and hard and the tip of it is tracing my balls. I shiver and say, 'Something cold… a CD…'" but she's already done that. She says, 'Come on, Andrew. Just guess.' And I can't do it."

I'm staring at him. The blue light casts flickering shadows over his handsome face. He's gone. Lost in the memory of it.

He says, "It's a knife. I mean, it's this big fucking knife, and I can't fucking say 'it's a knife,' because I don't want it to be a fucking knife," he pauses to breathe. "But one part of me does. I mean, one part of me is so fucking hot I'm gonna spurt all over her wrist and the blade and everything. And finally I just say, 'OK, it's a kitchen knife… get it away from me….' And she drops it and climbs on top of me and rides the living shit out of me, and we come together in the most amazing way."

He looks at me, waiting for my response. I'm in awe.

"Did you see it afterward?" I ask, curious. Aroused.

"I took off the blindfold and there it was, on the edge of the coffee table, this huge monster blade. And she's all smiles, saying it's a good thing she's got steady hands. But we never did it again. Not after that night. I never knew what she might do after that. What shit she might pull."

I grin at him, thinking about the things we might do… the things we're going to do… and I say, "Yeah, I understand."

"No," he says. "It was a knife. I mean, a *carving* knife.

Biggest fucking thing, ever."

Then he grabs me around the waist, slides off the leopard-print sheet, and pulls me up on top of him. We fuck again, in that eerie blue light, and I know both our minds are racing, trying to top it, trying to find the next higher level.

'Cause there's always one higher. Even when you reach the top.

Work In Progress

I realise now that at the beginning Colette was simply taking things slowly, being easy on such a wild stallion as myself. She thought if she moved too fast she might scare me off and into the arms of another, less-focused Mistress. And she was right. Had she spooked me with constant discipline, with too-soon, too-hard punishment, I would have fled. But instead, she teased me, taunted me, until I found myself begging her for it, asking her for it.

Standing in front of the refrigerator, reading over Mistress Julian's comments in a column cut from *Bad Girl*, feeling the heat and wetness start to flow at my core... that's when I began to understand the structure of a D/s relationship. Lowercase "s," always, head bowed, eyes lowered. Humble. I wasn't humble, clad in tight, black stretch pants and a lycra running top, my hair a jumble of windswept curls, my cheeks flushed from my morning run. I wasn't humble as I poured my juice into one of our vintage jelly glasses and prepared to make a single slice of toast.

Humble means getting Colette's meal first, bringing it on a tray to her bedroom, serving her with lowered eyes and then asking, in my softest voice, if there is anything else I can get for her. Humble means sitting on my heels on the floor by the bed, shoulders back, body arched, waiting for her to choose to feed me a bite of her toast, a bit of her muffin, a sip of her juice.

No, I was not humble. I was wild and spirited, unbroken and untamed. But I was searching. My day-job, my real-world, my nine-to-five life is perfect for that type of personality – though I lie, it's never nine-to-five, it's all-consuming.

I'm an artist, fairly successful for one so young, my work shown in many of the downtown galleries and quite a few of the private, wealthier estates in our community. I have a luminous quality to my art, they say, I have a free-flowing hand, a lack of inhibition when it comes to paints and brushes and colours in tubes. I have no fear of light or dark, of shading, of muting, of brightness, of screaming.

On the canvas, that is.

But alone, in bed, with my Mistress, I am out of control, all over the place, my strokes too heavy or too light, my body contorting in a vain effort to find peace. I need control here, where I have none. My breathlessness of art does not serve me well. My constant moving, shifting and gliding, my colours as they burst free – each one a different shade, a different hue – these take me further from my goal, not closer to it.

Colette sees this all, and she knows, and she ponders the best way there is to rein in a free spirit without damaging the soul. Her blue eyes flash with ideas, with concepts, but she doesn't rush into anything. She would not have me destroyed, she would not have the filament that glows inside me damaged, she would only have me tamed, when I am in her arms in bed. She would only have me find the peace that I so crave.

I used to be envious of those who possess that peace. I used to talk to girls on the bus who ferry themselves from job to home to TV dinners without so much as a thought to art or life or pleasure or pain. They were the lucky ones, I thought, without the need inside them that burns inside me. The fire that causes me to toss and turn restlessly in my Mistress' embrace – the inner rage that never lets up, that never finds its mark.

Sometimes, I'd talk to them, asking what they did for fun, flirting casually, easily, searching for the answer. Why were they so different? They seemed like creatures in a zoo, under glass, pinned down. I wanted to observe them, wanted to find out what was missing inside them that could enable them to enjoy watching soulless movies, empty TV, overly-bland theatrical performances. What was it? What was it?

Ah, maybe you've already guessed. It wasn't a lack in them, wasn't something they'd been born without, but something that I had been born with. Something that I had no control over, the heat, the fire, the need to create. And creating takes that extra bit and builds it up until it is a constant vein of life pulsing beneath the skin. You can't turn it on when you're in slump, you can't turn it off when you want to sleep. The paintings call you, the paintbrushes speak, the tubes of colour wake you up.

Come and create, they whisper. Forget food. Forget sleep. Forget love. Forget life. Come and make things of us. We need freedom. You can give us that freedom.

Doomed, head bowed, my Mistress is my art. She calls to me and I go. She beckons me, and I am hers. I walk on heavy feet to the studio and open the door. The light is just right, streaming through the window in curtains of yellow and gold. The paintings stand against the wall, mocking me, howling at me: finish us! What do you think you're doing? Sleeping? No sleep. No time. You don't have enough time.

There is too much art in my head.

It must come out.

Colette knows this, she strokes the side of my face when I sleep, she kisses my lips and tastes the life there, she uses a cool rag to wash the drips of paint from under my nails. She bathes me. She feeds me. She keeps my outer-workings in healthy order so that some day, sometime, I may find peace.

No peace while those voices call to me.

Come to the studio, there are ideas here. You can let them out. You can be free of them.

The stallion inside me bucks up and raises its head. I moan and look at the clock. "It's too early," I say to no visible creature. "Too early to start work."

"No," those voices chide at once. "It's too late."

I pull on my robe and wander to the studio, opening the door and staring at my works-in-progress. They call to me, like hungry children, feed me, finish me, use yourself up to make us whole. I find strength as I begin to mix the paints, my palette a ray of sin and light, of dark and heat, of wet and dry. I do not think in terms of colours, do not know the names of the tubes, but, instead, the feel of them in my hand. How much of this one has been used up, how much of that. The crinkly metal that folds and condenses, that looks so strong, but, once empty, is weak and brittle.

I gather my strength and I begin to paint, the moonlight playing melodies on my ghostly form. The sound of my feet as I shuffle on the wood floor a rhythm that matches my heart.

Colette knows – her blue eyes appear on my canvas, watching – Colette knows, and she tries, so hard, to understand. But she is not one of the artists, the few, the chosen, the cursed. She is not one of us. But she tries, she comes to stand in the doorway of the studio, her nightgown hanging long and loose down her body, her hair a tangle of gold spun from straw. She watches me work, never speaking, never interrupting, and I know – in a split second of wisdom – that she is as envious of me as I am of her.

She is complete, she is finished. She will never be anything but who she is.

While I … I am a work in progress.

Spanking Aphrodite

"I want you to practise with me," I begged Justine.

"What do you mean?" my friend asked, yelling to be heard over the music. We were at her annual pagan Halloween party, and the music was loud. I had on a toga and my black hair was loose down my back in my version of Aphrodite. A silly costume for me – Goddess of love? I don't think so. Justine was dressed like a nurse, and from the glances she was receiving, it looked as if several partiers were desperate for her to give them their yearly examination.

"I need to know what it's like first," I said, "you just don't understand."

"You're right," she said, "I don't understand at all."

Closing my eyes, I tried to think of how to explain. When I was in junior high school, I'd amazingly been the first of my friends to go to a school-sponsored dance. Amazingly, because I was so shy I could barely raise my hand in class. Once at the dance, I stood with my back solidly pressed against the wall, petrified. Finally, a boy I'd known since kindergarten, sidled up to me and asked what was wrong.

"I don't know how to dance," I confessed.

"There's nothing to it," Kevin told me, leading me to a dark corner of the gym. "All you need is practice." When the Police came on with *Every Little Thing She Does Is Magic*, he moved me to help me find the beat. He taught me how to move, shimmying and swaying in that dimly lit corner. Boys I'd turned down earlier in the evening stared at us. Why had I said yes to Kevin and no to them? It was an easy answer. He'd let me work it out before taking me to the centre of the room and dancing with all the other kids.

Now, squeezed on a sofa between my naughty nurse buddy and a friendly-looking Frankenstein, I told this story to Justine, trying to get her to comprehend what I wanted from her without having to actually spell it out. Justine took a sip of her drink and said, "You want me to dance with you? Should I search my CD collection for *Every Little Thing She Does Is Magic*?" I caught the sparkle in her eyes, though, and understood she was teasing me.

"Please," I said, and Justine seemed to stand up slightly straighter at the way I said it. Her buoyant breasts continued in their gravity-defying lifestyle, pointing straight at me.

"You want me to spank you," Justine said now, not asking, but telling. The Frankenstein looked my way and I blushed.

"It sounds ridiculous, I know. But I need to practise before I experience it with Antonia. That's just the way I am. If I don't know what it's like, I won't be able to let her do it to me. And she wants to spank me. She said so."

Justine grinned. "If you tell her afterwards, she'll probably punish you even more." I got the sense that she really enjoyed the image of Antonia disciplining me.

"Once I know, it won't be bad. It's the not knowing that kills me."

Justine shrugged. "I'll meet you in your apartment in

twenty minutes." Justine lowered her voice, "You're such a bad girl, Katrina. I never knew you had it in you."

And then she was downing the rest of her martini, stalking across the apartment to the hallway, and disappearing around the corner. I finished my own drink, then left the party, walking across the hall to my own apartment. I was very aware of how wet I was growing in anticipation of my first paddling. I didn't care if Antonia punished me worse. I had to know.

In my studio, I paced back and forth. From the bed to the window to the bed again. I stared at my reflection in the mirror on the back of the closet door. I saw my flushed cheeks, my trembling lower lip. I thought about how my father had taught me to drive, taking me anywhere I wanted to go ahead of time, so I could learn the route. Driving with me as the passenger first, then allowing me to take a turn behind the wheel. We drove in all kinds of weather: rain, wind, hail, until I was competent. This type of practice is ingrained into me. Try it out first. Test the waters. I'm the type of person who never just jumps into a swimming pool.

While waiting for my friend to arrive, I posed in front of the mirror. Then I turned around, lifted my dress, and took my panties down, and observed my naked ass. I pictured handprints decorating the pale, tender skin. I wondered if Justine would only play with me, or if she'd give it to me hard. If she'd make me cry. I tried to imagine exactly how much I could take before I cried.

Where was Justine? I wondered. I thought about calling her to ask what was taking her so long. Then I thought about calling her to cancel the whole thing, to tell her it all had been a joke, a sick joke, but I was over it now. What the fuck was I doing? Who was I trying to kid? I didn't have it in me, did I?

But even as that voice in my head tried to convince me to back out, I knew I wouldn't. My mind took me on a quick trip, visualizing Justine striding in on her amazing heels, standing right at the door and looking at me. Her curves barely reined in by the white nurse's outfit. The stethoscope still around her neck like some piece of alien-looking jewellery. I heard her telling me in her lilting voice that I'd been naughty, I'd been awfully naughty, and I was going to have a hard time sitting in the future. Telling me to lie face down on the bed and hug the pillow, that she'd be more than happy to mete out a bit of seriously-needed discipline to a wayward girl like me. That's what friends are for, right? To help out pals in need.

A knock at the door announced that Justine was finally coming to join me. I walked to the door and opened it, revealing not my neighbour... but Antonia, dressed handsomely in a cowgirl's costume, chaps over jeans, vest on over a tight, ribbed white tank, handkerchief tied around her neck. Her hair was tied back from her face. She looked like she'd stepped out of the wild west, and I scanned her body quickly, to make sure she wasn't holding a whip in her hand. What would I have done if she'd had one? Or a riding crop, or a quirt? And why did my panties get all clingy and wet at the thought? At the image of her riding me, the way someone would ride a hard-to-tame filly, her spurs digging into my sides.

"What...?" I started, confused, my mind trying to work quick enough to explain the situation to myself.

"Justine paged me," was all Antonia said at first, walking into the room in her black cowboy boots, forcing me to retreat toward the bed by her sheer presence. I didn't feel her hands on me, just her eyes, and they backed me up until I was against the edge of the mattress, until I sat down and then continued to scoot backward on the bed until my spine was pressed up against the headboard.

"She explained the situation," Antonia said. I tried to figure out how she'd gotten here so fast, imagined Justine paging Antonia at some Halloween fiesta downtown and saying, "Climb onto your Harley, kiddo, and get here now. Your brand-new girlfriend is ready for her first spanking. You wouldn't want to miss this."

But why wasn't Antonia saying anything? Why was she just looking at me like that? Because she wanted me to explain myself. Antonia waited. I looked her over. No, there was no weapon. No paddle. Looked closer. She had a worn leather belt coiled around her waist. While she waited for me, she stroked the silver buckle, started to undo it, to pull the sinuous black leather from the loops. Her movements were well-choreographed, and I leaned my head back against the wall and swallowed hard.

"Tell me about it, Katrina," Antonia said gently. "Tell me all about it."

Don't blow it this time, Katrina, I told myself. *Don't flail*. In my mind, I saw Kevin dancing with me under one stark bulb in the gymnasium. Moving to the music of the early 80s. Learning the steps before I had to work through them with someone else. Story of my life.

"I wanted to know," I said, finally, watching her fold the belt in her hands, double the leather up between both hands and snap it. The sound was louder than I expected, but I was proud that it didn't make me jump. I just stared at her and waited for her response. Without speaking, she undressed me, a simple feat seeing as I had on only a white, diaphanous toga-style dress. She left me in my silky panties, stepping back to appreciate the way I looked before sitting on the edge of the bed and dragging me across her lap.

"Look over there," she said, indicating the mirror on the wall across the room. I looked. I saw. "Tell me the rest," she said, pulling my panties down my thighs, but leaving them there, making me feel more naked for that little bit of fabric around my ankles. More naked, more exposed, more naughty.

"Tell me," Antonia said, slightly louder. "I'm not going to ask you again."

She knew all the answers, but she still wanted to hear me confess. "Justine was going to practise with me," I said, the words coming out in a rush. It felt good to come clean, even if she already knew what I was going to say. It seemed that saying it was the important part.

Her hand slapped against my skin. Connecting once. Hard. That sound. I shuddered. I wanted this. Why did I want this? Why did I need it, crave it, desire it so badly that my body was shaking all over? Why couldn't I shut my mind off, shut the voice off in my head that insisted on analysing the situation, continuing to analyse it as she continued to spank me. Just using her hand now, not her belt, which I could see in the reflection, coiled menacingly at her side on the white comforter.

"Why couldn't you trust me?" she asked, rubbing the heel of her palm over my sparking hot flesh, pressing hard where the violet-tinged handprints were already standing out in stark relief. I wondered if her handprints would leave marks, handsome beet-coloured bruises. I wondered if, afterward, I could stand in front of the mirror and look at my ass, reddened and pretty – yes, I thought it would be pretty – admire it. Would those prints last?

"Why?" she asked again, and then, in a softer voice, "you need to start answering me when I ask you a question. That's the first rule you should memorize."

"I do trust you," I said, my voice not sounding at all like my voice. Lying. I was lying to her now. What was I thinking? Upturned, over her lap, her sturdy thighs below me, her hand now truly punishing my blushing skin. She spanked me to make it hurt. Lying wasn't getting me anywhere, was it? Sure it was, because I wanted this, and lying was going to get me exactly what I wanted, as quick as anything else I could imagine.

But still, my voice, that inner chastising voice would not be quiet. My mind wondered what Justine had said on the phone. "Come here quick and spank my naughty friend." The thought horrified me, and how had Antonia responded. Shut up! I screamed inside my mind. Lose yourself in this, because this is what you want. Pay attention to your fantasy as it comes to life.

"Bad girl," Antonia said between clenched teeth. "Come clean with me."

Her hand was now wrapped around the belt. The cool metal buckle pressed deep into my hot skin. I stayed silent, watching her hand come back, move high up, and then forward in a blur, the leather slapping against my ass as hard as anything I could imagine.

I didn't know what to say.

Somehow Antonia understood this. Pushing me off her lap, she stood and walked to the dresser, pulled it opened and grabbed a pair of my nylons from the top drawer. She came back to the bed and quickly bound my wrists above my head. Threw me back down on the bed, on my stomach, my head on the pillow, her body behind me. I hadn't known she'd be so strong. Hoped it, perhaps, but hadn't known it. Though I should have, right? I should have known from her stories of scaling the walls at the climbing gym, of scaling the mountains in the desert outside of L.A. Strong upper body, tensed muscles ready beneath the skin.

When I was tied to the bed, my arms were fastened over my head with silken bindings and my legs were spread wide apart, my ankles tied, as well, she stood before me. She looked untamed. and intense, as if she were nowhere else but in this room, in this moment, with me at her total mercy.

Being tied was hard for me. Harder than I would have thought. In fact, it was the opposite of what I would have thought. Bound to the bed should have been easier, since I had no choice in the matter. Instead, I felt as if my brain were going a hundred miles a minute, while my body was unfairly contained. I couldn't get away, and she knew it. I had nowhere to go but down.

I kept silent, watching her pick up the belt and play with it between her hands. "Don't you trust me, Katrina?"

I nodded.

"That's important," she said, "you need to trust your partner when you enter into a relationship like this one. A relationship that is based on power and rules. That's the second thing you should memorize. The concept behind what we have. The balance of our connection. Do you understand that?"

I nodded again.

"Say it."

"I understand."

"I thought we would have started differently," Antonia said, her voice holding a note of faux sadness. "A ride on the back of my Harley to get you wet and drippy and vibrating. Instead, we'll go at it a different way –"

The belt was still in her hand, but now she stood to the side of me and I could not watch, could not see it in the mirror anymore. And in this new position, she plunged me into pain. The belt connected with my burning skin. Once. Twice. Three times. With these few strokes, she striped my ass, my upper thighs. Then she paused and said, her voice low and powerful, "You'll get the pleasure part later, you know. You'll feel all of it later. But I want you to know, now, right now, what it feels like to be punished. Seriously punished."

She lined up the blows right next to each other. She was good at this. I was conscious enough to think that before my mind turned off, that voice turned off, finally and as concretely as if I'd turned down the volume on my stereo. And I let myself be washed in the fire of it, the thrill of it, pulled for once out of fantasies and into the absolute present with each stroke of her belt.

In all honesty, I can't say what I was thinking during the thrashing. I know that it hurt, and that it hurt in a way that no pain has ever hurt before. Thinking back, it made me remember the time when Justine got her first tattoo. Standing outside on Sunset, I asked her how it felt, even though I'd seen her grit her teeth through it, sitting by her side in the back of The Sunset Strip Tattoo Parlour. Watching her hold her breath each time the needle came close to her skin. Listening when the tattoo artist said, "Relax for me. Breathe for me." Justine had told me, "It hurt…"

"But how much?"

"You can't compare it to anything," she had said matter-of-factly. "I wanted it, so it hurt in an entirely different way than any other type of pain."

That's what this was like. I wanted it. The pain was astounding, but I bore it because I wanted it. The belt on my skin hurt in an entirely different way than anything I'd ever felt. Antonia strode onward, I'm sure knowing instinctively how much I could take. Not pushing me to the limits, but pushing me to the first ridge. She gave me everything I wanted, and everything I needed.

Even after only really knowing me a short time, she knew my innermost cravings. Antonia rewarded me with lines that I could admire later, standing in front of the mirror and looking over my shoulder at my ass and thighs. She gave me memories, so that when I pressed my fingers into those berry-striped marks, I could immediately call up the pain of the moment, step right back into the feeling of being tied, of being her captive. She gave me every fantasy, every daydream, night dream, yearning desire come true.

"No more games," Antonia said, when she was finished. Finished with the punishment portion, anyway. She pressed her body against mine, her clothed body, thighs in chaps, against my naked one. "No more tests and no more games."

"Yes," I said softly. "I promise."

Antonia wrapped her arms around me, letting me feel the bulge in her slacks where she was packing, moving back to undo her fly and let me actually feel the synthetic cock against my throbbing flesh. Rubbing back and forth against me. This was real. This was here and now, as she wet the tip of it between my legs, as she pulled back once, then plunged inside.

She sighed when my wetness met with her skin, with the lower part of her belly, with the hidden lips of her pussy. She sighed because it was proof positive that she and I were matched, that the way she had taken care of the situation was perfect for us both. The deep stroking of her cock inside me made me moan. She pushed it in and pulled it out, and I shivered and squeezed against her synthetic tool.

"That's right," she said, "that's the girl. Fuck it for me. Make it happen. I need you to make it happen."

I needed it to happen, too, and I did just as she told me. Embracing the dildo with my cunt, I held onto it, trying to keep her inside me even as she pulled back, teasing me, taunting me. Each stroke of her cock made me once and truly, finally whole. She pressed into me until her thighs were against my thighs, the flatness of her belly against my ass. She pounded into me, saying over and over, under her breath, "Make it happen, girl. Reach for it."

I reached. I pushed. My eyes squeezed shut tightly, echoing the contractions of my pussy. Her hand came down between us, tickling fingers finding my clit, slipping up and down on either side. And finally, when I thought I wouldn't be able to take any more, when I felt strung out and beat up from her driving cock, I came.

"That's the girl," she said, sensing the exact moment. "Perfect girl, my perfect girl." Her hands stroked my naked body, fingertips trailing over me, running up and down my spine. She let her nails bite into my skin and I shuddered, still coming as she pulled out, unbuckled her harness, rubbed her pussy against my dripping cunt. Antonia came that way, her delta of Venus against mine, bumping and rubbing until she reached her climax, holding onto me tightly, biting into my shoulder as the waves took her away.

When we were finished, after I'd spent long minutes wrapped in her arms, she untied me, and I rolled over to look up at her. She stroked my face gently, her fingers warm on my hot skin. Then she bent down and kissed my lips, deeply kissed me until I was hungry for more, desperate for more, whether it meant more pain or more pleasure, I no longer cared. They were entwined in my mind. One and the same.

High Tea

4:00 p.m. Thursday. Dainty ceramic tea pot nestled beneath a white crocheted warmer. Sterling silver service polished to a reflecting sheen. Antique lace tablecloth so fine it could tear if you looked at it too hard.

Last place on fucking earth you'd find my boyfriend Charlie.

His gold-flecked eyes are wide open, and he tosses his long, glossy-black hair out of his face with an impatient shrug. "You're kidding, right?" he asks, visibly flinching when I tell him what I want.

"An array of delicacies served to us in our own suite by a private waiter well-schooled in the age-old ritual of high tea," I continue, undaunted by his expression. I am repeating a passage from the slick brochure of one of San Francisco's most famous – and snobby – hotels. A passage that has turned me on indescribably.

Charlie just stares, dark brows arched incredulously. *What have I done with his girlfriend?* his expression says. *And who is this Martha Stewart-like impostor who has taken her place?*

"You won't regret it," I assure him, and he finally reads the look in my green eyes correctly, because he begrudgingly nods his okay. Promised pleasure will make people do the most unusual things.

4:15. Thursday. The tuxedoed waiter has left, and Charlie is a true believer. Fantasy feast of finger-length cucumber and cream cheese sandwiches are ignored in favour of a far more decadent fantasy. Tiny tea cakes sit iced so prettily all alone. And my man is spread out on the richly carpeted floor, tan slacks open, receiving his first-time-ever tea-flavoured blow job.

"Oh, God, Julie. Take another sip."

The fragrant liquid fills my mouth and I hold it for a second, swishing slightly before swallowing. Then I'm back down on him, my lips hot from the Earl Gray, the welcoming sensation of a pre-warmed mouth caressing his rock-hard rod. Sip, swallow, and suck. We could do this all day.

"Too good," Charlie groans and arches his slim hips, pressing forward, gaining the contact he craves. "More. Please –"

Pinkie in the air, I drink again, taking my time to savour the flavour, a combination now of the strong tea and the hot-summertime taste of my boyfriend's naked skin. I am wearing sleek white gloves and a ruffled pastel party dress in place of my standard uniform of faded Levis, turtleneck sweater, and beat-up black leather jacket. But my soft caramel hair has come down from its too-tight bun, and I feel that my perfectly applied lipstick has smeared. No outfit has ever excited me more.

Charlie's warm brown eyes burn me with their heat as I swallow the tea, and then he stands, strips out of clothes, and gets ready to really play. Gripping onto my shoulders, he moves my body, so that I'm on my back and he's positioned above me, thrusting hard and slow into my willing, waiting mouth. I look up at him, at the tribal tattoos that criss-cross his broad biceps, at the silver hoops piercing his nipples. He's comfortable cruising the steepest city hills on his Ducati. Or spread underneath his treasured old Chevy pick-up with his battered toolbox nearby. He's at ease in dangerous places that would scare every upper-crust guest in this elite hotel.

And now he's turned on by tea time.

When his cock presses against the back of my throat, I reach one hand up to find his balls as he sets the rhythm of the ride. The light caress of my still-gloved fingers takes Charlie to a higher level.

"That, Julie," he whispers urgently. "Keep doing that."

My fingertips make gentle circles as my mouth sucks harder. Careful rotations of soft fabric against even softer skin. The two differing sensations make Charlie close his eyes and moan, thrusting even harder and then holding still. Sealing himself to me. I'm growing wetter beneath the silly ruffles of the dress, and I look up from my position on the floor and see pink-orange sunlight filtering through the scalloped lace edge of the tablecloth.

It's going to be a long afternoon.

Four-ish. Every Thursday. Our place.

We own our own mismatched tea service now, purchased for pennies at a second-hand store. And a small selection of teas resides in our cabinet, seemingly out of place near the bottles of exotic tequila and Johnnie Walker Black Label. Charlie sets the scene himself, his large hands working to stay calm as he envisions the pleasures that await him. Delicate tea cups rattle on their saucers. Petite cookies jump on the plate as he sets it onto the tray.

I put one hand on his to slow him, and then we partake in the ritualistic and aristocratic pleasure of high tea.

Bad Girl

My ex-boyfriend and I used to play a game that seemed so naughty to me, I still blush at the thought. I'm sure other people have done worse, and I'm sure some folks will think it was nothing to feel guilty about. But to me, it was as if we'd crossed a line, some line of decency. After we played this game I would look at Paul with an expression of stunned satisfaction, pleased that we'd escaped a thunderbolt once again.

It's not that we were normally tame. From the beginning, Paul and I had a fairly wild sex life. He was a teacher at a high school in town, and we made love on his desk after the kids had left for the day. He spanked me. He tied me up. We fucked in public. I sucked him off while he drove. I fucked him at his mother's house. At a Christmas party, he took my cup of coffee into the bathroom, came into it, and brought it back to me. While I drank, he stood across the room, staring, excited to the point where he could no longer make idle conversation with those around him. These activities paled in comparison to our brand new game.

It started while on vacation in the northern part of California. He'd rented a stone cabin in one of those old-fashioned vacation parks. There were twelve other cabins in the resort, all carefully spread out beneath a scattering of redwoods so that you felt as if you had the whole forest to yourself. Our little bungalow contained two beds, a small living area, and a kitchen. For some reason, and I still don't know why, I climbed into one bed and Paul climbed into the other. Maybe it's because it had been such a long day driving. Maybe we were just playing around, as if we weren't going to fuck that night – unlikely for us. I rolled over, facing the wall, and stared at the pattern of the stones. Several minutes went by before Paul stood up and lifted the covers on my bed. As he climbed in next to me, he said, "Shhh, angel, we don't want Mommy to hear."

I froze. This wasn't our normal type of game. When we did s/m, he would talk dirty to me. He might say, "Lisa, you've been a bad girl, haven't you? Bad girls get spanked. Hold onto your ankles, and don't you stand up. Don't you flinch." He was the dominant, but he was always just Paul, my handsome boyfriend. If I played the role of a younger me, I was still me.

Now, he said, "You be a good girl. You be nice for Daddy." I stayed totally still. His hands wandered between my legs, touching me through my panties, tracing the outer lips of my vagina. It felt good and bad and confusing, and I drenched my underwear. "Uh oh," he said, "my little girl's all wet for me. Did you get yourself all wet for Daddy? Is that what you did?"

I couldn't answer. I just let him keep touching and stroking and playing. When he pressed up against my leg and I felt his hard cock, I thought that alone was going to make me come, that insistence of his cock brushing against my thigh.

"We have to be really quiet, Lisa," he said softly. "Mommy's asleep in the other bed, and we don't want to wake her. Then she'd know what I know. She'd know just what a bad girl you are. What a sinful little girl you are. I'd have to punish you severely if she ever found that out. Do you understand me?"

I nodded.

"Good girl," he said, "That's my good girl."

He spooned against me, lifting my nightgown, lowering my panties, and entering me from behind. His hands wandered over the front of my nightgown, cupping my breasts. He pressed his lips to my ear, whispering, "My girl is getting so big now, isn't she? Look at the way your breasts fill my hands." He rubbed my nipples against the flat of his palms and they stood at attention, poked against the flannel fabric of my nightgown. "Yes, she is. Nice and big for me. And look at how hard your little nips get. I only have to brush them lightly."

His voice was this husky whisper, as if he were honestly trying to keep quiet. His cock throbbed inside me, and he brought one hand to the front of my body, raising my nightgown and placing his fingers against my pussy. He pressed against me, finding the wetness, then locating my clit and sliding his fingers over it and around it. I moaned at that sensation, and instantly he hissed, "Didn't I say to be quiet? We're going to have to go outside behind the house for a little punishment session if you can't control yourself. Look over on that chair, Lisa." I turned my head slightly. "See Daddy's belt?" I murmured an assent. "I'm going to have to tan your bottom with that belt if you can't keep yourself under control. You know what that feels like, don't you, girl? Don't you know what it feels like to have your bottom thrashed by my belt?"

His fingers played me. They stroked up and down, and I tried so hard to do what he said, to be quiet and behave. I'd never been that turned on before. Not when he used mailing tape to bind me over one of the little desks in his classroom, slapping the wooden ruler on my naked haunches. Not when we snuck off at his sister's wedding and fucked during the reception. This was it. My pinnacle. The dirtiest thing I could think of, and it made me weak. I didn't moan again, but my breathing came hard and fast.

"You need to be quiet," he said in that hushed, menacing tone. "Daddy gets so tired of having to punish you. Why can't you be a good girl, Lisa? Why can't you be good for me, like your sister?"

That did it. That made me come. Sick and twisted and over the top, I leaned back against him and let the rip tide of orgasm slam through me. He gripped his arms around me, bucking faster and faster until he reached it, too, pulling out to come all over my backside, holding me tight so I couldn't turn around to face him, to see whatever expression of horror on his face would reflect my own. What had we done? What had we just done? What line did we cross? Where would we go from here?

"Bad girl," was all he said, lips against my ear. "I always knew you were a really bad girl, Lisa. And bad girls get punished. Why don't you go over there and get my belt so we can deal with this? Go on and get it for me. You know you deserve it, Lisa." He shook his head. "Such a bad little girl."

Bad girl, I thought as I stood and walked to the chair. That's what I am. That's what I was the whole time, I just hadn't known it for sure.

Sailor Boy

To me, the term "macho" means masculine. Powerful. Butch. Given this definition, the word doesn't even begin to describe my husband, Alexander. Tall and strong, he has a deep, commanding voice that resonates when he talks, vibrates inside my head when he says my name. I like to watch him move, to watch him stride. When he cuts through a crowd, people move out of his way.

Before we met, Alexander was a commercial fisherman, spending eight rough years at work on a variety of vessels. He lived thirty days at sea at a time, followed by one week breaks on land. He credits his time aboard ship for building his spirit, his mind, his body. At sea, Alex came across as the toughest of the bunch. There were no women on the fishing boats – chicks on board are considered bad luck – and there was no sexual activity among the men. At least, none that anyone would admit to if they wanted to be hired for a second trip. To get the reputation for liking guys meant instant unemployment in the fishing game. But while Alex fulfilled his he-man duties, he lost himself in a forbidden fantasy. One that didn't come true until he met me.

Many husbands give their wives perfume on February 14th, but my handsome sailor boy gave me something with a twist. Not Chanel Number Five, Joy, or Anaïs

Anaïs, but a fancy brand of men's cologne. "Happy Valentine's Day, Becky," he whispered as I tore through the heart-printed wrapping paper to reveal the expensive bottle. I looked at it, looked at Alex, and smiled. I knew exactly what my one true love wanted from Cupid, and I wasn't about to let him down.

Alex has grey-green eyes that change when he stares at me. They grow darker, more turbulent, like a storm at sea. As I began to rub the spicy lotion into the soft skin at the base of my throat, his eyes shimmered with desire and longing.

"Get undressed," I said, motioning with my chin toward the bedroom. "Strip out of your clothes and then wait for me."

He couldn't hide his grin, but he ducked his head, bashfully, and then followed my command. Wives tend to know their husbands, sometimes better than the men know themselves. I'd been planning for this day for a long time, and I felt excitement pool within me. What a surprise Alex was in for – he thought he knew the evening's plans, but he had no idea. After he'd left the room, I stood and got the secret present I'd been saving for him. Quickly, I pulled out the leather harness and dildo, then grabbed an outfit from the back of the hall closet and went into the bathroom to change. Or, rather, to *transform*.

With Alex's unfulfilled fantasy in mind, I had purchased a vintage sailor suit at a second-hand store. It was white with a black anchor on the sleeve and a musky, male smell to the fabric, even though I'd had it dry-cleaned. I hung the outfit on the back of the door while I attached the moulded cock-shaped dildo to the harness, then slid the straps on and buckled the leather belt around my waist. The cock was as true-to-life as they come, as close to my actual skin colour as possible, and ribbed with realistic veins. In length and girth it matched Alex's almost exactly, which was what I'd wanted. My desire was for him to experience what I get to feel every night.

After admiring my cock in the mirror, and admonishing myself not to get too infatuated with the look of it, I slid into the outfit. First, I put on a tight, white tank bra that pressed my small breasts flat to my chest. I pulled the top over my head and then tried on the pants. I'm a slim 5'8", but I'd had the pants altered and they fit perfectly, showing off the newfound bulge in front and my fine, round ass in the back. As I dressed, I imagined Alex's hands unbuttoning the fly, his trembling fingers revealing the moulded cock concealed beneath. One that was destined to introduce his virgin ass to the as yet unexperienced pleasures of life as a submissive.

I completed my outfit with a pair of beat-up black Doc Martens. Then I slicked my short, blonde hair away from my face and gave myself a final once-over. It was my intention to look the part of a boy, yet retain my feminine side, and I felt as if I'd done a perfect job. Still, I took my time with my finishing touches, sure that Alex was squirming in our room, growing harder every second. He's unused to being out of control, tends to take charge in our relationship – at least, in the bedroom portion of it. I wondered what he was thinking about, whether his heart was beating extra fast from that sexy combination of anticipation and fear.

With more swagger to my stride than normal, I walked out of the bathroom and down the hall to our bedroom. Alex likes to tease me, says that I always walk as if I'm going somewhere, even when we're out for a leisurely stroll. Now, I definitely had a purpose. Each step brought me further into my character. Long ago, Alex had confessed to being attracted to one of the cooks who had worked on a boat with him. He claimed the boy had looked like me, was of a slighter build than the rest of the burly sailors, with fairly feminine features and a "divine ass". So, now I was Jake Miller, heading into our room to turn a forbidden fantasy into a reality.

I opened the door slowly, seeing that Alex had dimmed the lights and lit the two ivory candles on our dresser. He was sitting on the edge of the bed, wearing a pair of grey, cotton boxers, his eyes lowered, his body shaking slightly. I'd never seen him nervous before, never imagined he could appear vulnerable. Now that he was, I had a momentary lapse back into myself, wanting to go on my hands and knees in front of him, take his face in my hands, croon soothing words. But I'd fail him if I did.

Instead, I approached solidly, grabbed his chin in my hand and forced him to meet my eyes. He didn't want to. He raised his face but kept his eyes lowered, staring at my feet.

"Look at me," I said, my voice low and as gruffly masculine as possible. His body shivered again, and this time he obeyed. "I've seen you watching me," I told him, "seen the way you stare when I walk by. You think about me at night, alone in your bunk, your hand on your cock."

Alex swallowed hard and nodded. My confidence grew inside me. I could feel a heat spreading through my chest.

"You work yourself and imagine that I'm fucking you."

Again, he nodded, his eyes wide. Taking a step closer, I pressed the bulge of my hidden rod directly in front of his mouth.

"You want to taste my cock, don't you?" I asked, my tone still low, barely louder than a whisper.

"Yeah." His mouth was partly open. He looked as if he wanted to deep throat me right there. I didn't let him, but I rubbed my pants-clad cock against his mouth, taunting him with the tool. He opened his mouth wider, cupping the head of my cock between his lips, wetting the clothing of my pants with his saliva. He looked as if he knew what he was doing, and I felt a surge of wetness in my pussy beneath the plastic prick. I was getting turned on watching his grey eyes beg me.

"Unbutton my fly," I told him, savouring the look of gratitude that flickered across his face. He was quick to oblige, undoing the buttons and then sliding the pants down my hips so that my cock bulged forward. That wasn't good enough for me. I kicked out of the shoes and tore off the pants, so that I had better control of my cock. What a perfect specimen it was, everlastingly erect and ready.

"Suck me," I ordered next, the words not even out of my mouth before his lips were around my new toy. I stroked his soft, auburn hair while he made good use of his mouth. I felt the pull of his throat muscles as he tried futilely to drain a plastic cock.

"This is going in your ass," I told him next, and he sighed out loud, around the dildo. "This is going deep in your ass, and you're gonna cry out with each stroke. You're going to whimper like a girl." I didn't know where the words were coming from, but I let them come, did nothing to stifle myself. In reality, there's no way I can force Alex to do anything. He outweighs me by over 50 pounds, but I just let my body and my mind get into it, not caring that our heights and weights were so disproportionate to the characters we were playing. And as I pulled him off me and motioned for him to take off his boxers and get face-down on the bed, I could tell I'd have no back-talk from him. He wanted this. He'd been fantasizing about it for years.

There was a tube of K-Y in the drawer (I'd planned ahead), and I lubed both my cock and his asshole before introducing him to the toy. Gently, I pressed the head of the cock into his asshole, giving him just the first inch. His body tensed, the muscles in his back alive and straining. His head twitched on the pillow, and I could see his reflection in the glass-encased picture over our bed. He was biting his lip, trying to stop himself from moaning.

But I wanted him to moan.

I thrust into him with the full length of the cock, then pulled out quickly, and jogged right back in. Don't ask me how I knew the rhythm, or how I sensed what he needed. I just knew. The way to please my husband was to fuck him hard, to fuck him fast. He wanted to be taken, and I had no problem delivering.

Within a few strokes, he simply couldn't help himself. He leaned his head back and groaned at the feel of it, the intrusion and the sensation of being filled. I liked making him lose himself, and I wanted to keep up the ride. Squatting on my knees on either side of his body, I came back up on my feet for better control. I have very strong thigh muscles, and I used them to really fuck him. Grabbing onto his shoulders for support, I slammed into him with the cock, speaking the whole time, saying, "You like it like that, don't you Alex? You like it when your boyfriend fucks your ass…"

I took his moans for assents, not asking him to answer me properly. He was so lost in his daydreams, that I don't think he would even have heard me if I'd made a demand. Somewhere else in his mind, he was being fucked by his fantasy sailor boy. But I felt no competition. I'm the woman he comes home to, the woman he comes into, and I leaned my body against his and took a deep breath, smelling the cologne more strongly now that my body was growing hotter. Three fragrances permeated the room: the scent of Aramis, the scent of sweat, and the scent of sex.

Alex controlled the rhythm when he was about to climax, taking over from me and bucking his hips against the sheets, forcing himself back onto the whole of my cock, fucking himself with it. He sighed as he came, calling me Jake, and then calling me Becky, and then smiling as he rolled over and murmuring again, "Happy Valentine's Day…"

"Happy Valentine's Day, baby," I whispered back, knowing that we wouldn't wait for a special occasion to play this kind of game again.

The Sweets Of San Francisco

San Francisco is known for many things: the towering Golden Gate Bridge, the rich dark chocolate, the curvaceous hills, the vibrator museum. But to my way of thinking, the most important landmark can't be found on any map of classic tourist sites. Eat your heart out with jealousy, because it's mine alone to enjoy – that special no-man's region between my girlfriend's thighs.

I'm not only talking about her sweet pussy, although I must say that her cunt is my all-time, five-star favourite place to dine. No, my road map of pleasure starts much lower on Miranda's body. Generally, I begin a bit a bit above her knees but well below the curves of her inner thighs. I lick my way up her legs, giving her time to both tune in and turn on. There's nothing like it. Moving my tongue in slow strokes up her soft skin. Lapping with the flat of my tongue, then tracing designs with the pointed tip.

I can sense her pleasure as it starts to build. She wriggles her body on the mattress, or the sofa, or the linoleum-covered floor of our kitchen. She moans softly and makes encouraging cat-like noises, little half-purrs, half-growls.

But even more arousing to me than her sounds or her actions is her scent. It wafts over me slowly, creeps up on me like San Francisco's famous early morning fog. I wait for it as my tongue takes the trip along her body. All my senses are in tune, preparing for the first heady breath of her pussy. Each time, it's the same. That scent makes my own cunt throb in response, echoing her pleasure.

"Tomi," she whimpers. "Please –"

There is no word following please. This is because she doesn't want me to stop or to go faster. Truly, Miranda doesn't want me to do anything except exactly what I'm doing. Licking my way ever so slowly toward the split between her thighs, and taking my time to enjoy the view along the way. Still, she can't stay quiet because… well, because she can't.

The smoothness of her shaved skin reaches up and up to her completely bare pussy. It's so different from the wild woolliness between my own legs. I love that difference, like to nuzzle my nose up into it, letting her feel every part of my face with her cunt. I do this before I even part my lips for the first taste, before I introduce her to the wetness of my tongue at her core.

When I'm ready – and we go by my speed and by my clock – I breathe in deeply, like someone at a wine tasting inhaling the bouquet. The scent of her pussy is like nothing else, and like everything else. It is like a deep, French Merlot. A lemon-fresh breeze. A first sip of strong espresso. More than that, it's addictive. I simply can't get enough.

That's all right with Miranda. She doesn't want me to get enough. Parting her slender thighs wider to help, she runs her fingers through my tousled, grey-streaked hair. Tonight, we are in the kitchen because occasionally I like to play in the stark atmosphere as a change from the comfort of our bed. The bedroom is Miranda's domain, with her flurry of fluffed-up pillows, goose-down comforter, satin sheets. But the kitchen is all mine and it matches my clear-headed personality: stainless steel sink, sleek chopping knives perfectly displayed, neatly stacked plates. I like to see my rose-cheeked girlfriend naked on the black-and-white chequered floor, her hands over her head, her blue eyes half-shut in a look of total bliss.

Miranda is completely stripped, but I'm still in jeans and a white T-shirt, leather boots on, leather belt around my waist. Being dressed while she's nude turns me on even more, and I have to scoop her ass up in my hands, lift her hips to my mouth and feed. Even though I've worked at a lazy pace to this point, now I feel that heat pulse within me. I want to drink her down. Want to swallow her up.

My face presses tight against her pussy. My tongue flicks deep inside. I lick and lick, tickling her clit with just the tip before driving it in home. I am sealed to her cunt, but I still can hear her speak. "Tomi," she says, and I hear in the tone of her voice how close she is. Teetering. But I already knew that from the abundant juices smeared across my lips.

"Oh, God, Tomi, yes –" she moans, reaching down again to twine her fingers in my hair as she comes. Pushing hard. Pulling in. I lap at her dripping slit until those magic waves crest through her. Until she's breathless and limp in my arms.

The sweets of San Francisco.

That's what my girlfriend is. And just like any sinful dessert, I cannot get enough.

Search And Replace

I am a straight woman. A gay male. A lesbian. I like bondage. Orgies. The romance of flower petals. Spankings turn me on. I always wear racy lingerie. Leather makes me wet. I've made love on deserted moonlit beaches. Done it at a drive-in movie. Fucked in S & M clubs.

"You must have amazing sex," my best friend drunkenly gushed at me once at a party. There was a wistfulness in her voice.

Oh, I do. You have no idea.

But it's all in my head.

As a writer, I easily play out my fantasies. Close my eyes, think of something that excites me, then scribble it down in my ever-present notebook. Later, I transcribe the words onto my laptop, polishing and changing. In this manner, I have been tied up, blindfolded, dressed in shiny vinyl and six-inch spiked heels. Lovers have told me everything I ever wanted to hear because I have created all the dialogue myself. There is power in being a writer. You can make people say things and do things. And you can play all the parts by yourself. How fucking sexy is that?

Changing sexual preference is simple, too. As quick as typing a "search and replace" command into a file on the computer. Men become women with a few key strokes. A hetero encounter can transform into a luscious lesbian love affair. Names change from "Joe" to "Jill." Cocks turn to strap-ons. Emotions are the same. It's the body parts that need tweaking.

Reality, of course, is a whole different game. I always knew that in my mind, but I didn't truly understand it until recently. Yes, over the years I've written thousands of pages about women with women, threesomes, foursomes, S/M and b/d. Name the kink and I have played it out on paper to the extreme. In real life? I am an amateur.

When you think "pornographer" you probably don't picture someone like me. I'm small and quiet, with sleek, blonde hair that falls past my shoulders and the type of creamy pale skin that people refer to as "milk fed." I blend easily into a crowd, which is perfect for my means. I like to spy, to listen in, to gather information. Stories are all around me. I only need to pay attention. Rarely do I join the fun. It's unnecessary for me to actually experience the things that my characters do, all the filthy sexy things, because I live a double life on paper.

Unnecessary, at least, until I met Eleanor.

My characters will behave the way that I tell them. Eleanor wouldn't. When we went out together, she pressed herself against me, her body long and lean, hot and demanding. In bars, in lines at clubs, on the dance floor, her delicate fingers would stroke the back of my neck, taunting me with her touch. If I turned to look at her, she'd grin in innocence and refuse to comment. Eleanor followed no rules. Uncontrollable, she teased and flirted, pushed me to my limits, made me break out of my watching persona and respond to her overtures.

As we sipped drinks together in Hollywood's dark and

smoky Kitten's Dressing Room, she put her hand firmly on my thigh and moved it higher and higher until her probing fingertips had disappeared beneath the laced-edge hem of my short black skirt.

"You like that?" she asked as she stroked along the silky seam of my panties.

I swallowed hard, then took a deep breath. Maybe she'd continue to play the lead, let me know how to act by following her overtures. But no, Eleanor would have none of that. If I was going to be with her, then I had to commit to it.

My hand around the glass of gin and tonic trembled. A bit of the alcohol spilled over the rim and I licked at my wrist to gather the drops. Eleanor said, "I like the way you look when you do that."

"What?" I asked, thinking *"Spill my drink?"*

"Lick," she said. "I like the way you look when you lick –"

At her words, I instantly knew what it would feel like to nestle between her legs and run my tongue in one long line up the inside of her thighs. I knew it, because I'd been there before, on paper. But now, without a script, I had no idea how to get to that magical place. The helpful redheaded bartender moved to our corner and handed me a folded paper napkin. I dabbed at the liquor, using anything as an excuse not to meet Eleanor's deep brown eyes.

I'm not, I should insert here, a virgin. And I'm not brand-new to girl-girl scenes. At nineteen, I had my first threesome with a woman from my office and her beautiful male roommate. Back then, I let other people lead and I followed. Followed Amanda into her bed, let her choreograph every moment of that amazing eye-opening evening. She was older. She set the stage. And I think she liked being in charge. Besides that, youngsters can get away with being followers. At thirty, I now possessed a will and an opinion of my own. Eleanor wanted to hear what I had to say.

I turned to look at our reflections in the blue-tinted mirror behind the bar. There, I saw heat in Eleanor's eyes, the yearning, but nothing else. I could find no answer in our mirrored selves to help me out. No clues. No hints. Eleanor was still waiting, and I was failing her.

The band took up the stage again, a rollicking group of four motley musicians with one hit song and twenty losers. Immune or simply numb to the sad quality of the music, people made their way to the chequered dance floor and moved to the steady beat. Eleanor would dance with me if I asked her. She was wearing a vibrant red dress, and with her short, chestnut hair and panther-lean body, she reminded me of an Amazon. Gilded gold skin, lovely brown eyes, small breasts. We'd look amazing out there together. Her dark and my light, matching like shadows. Attached, touching, connected.

But this overworked mind of mine wouldn't let me act. Instead, I had to think about each stage, to plan and process. Eleanor waited so patiently, lifting her martini and taking a sip, turning slowly on the barstool to watch the band demolish a cover of my favourite Stones song, 'Miss You'.

Finally, I stood and looked at my friend.

"Let's get out of here."

"Where?"

"Your place," I said. There was too much history in mine. History of past lovers and ghost lovers and lovers from my books. Men and women. Singular and plural. I wanted a clean page, wanted a room that I hadn't created myself either in real life or in fiction.

Eleanor laced her fingers in mine and we walked out of the bar together, neither one of us taking the lead. The drive to her penthouse apartment was almost silent. Down Doheny to Beverly to her place across La Brea. As we entered her apartment, Eleanor moved to light candles, and the room took on a warmth. A perfect, shimmering glaze. Her bed was too far away for us. We made love on the floor of the living room, on her white rug, in front of her fireplace. For once, I didn't have to think. As soon as I touched her, I knew. Knew how to unzip her dress and slide it off her body. Knew how to kiss along the line of her spine until I reached the dimpled indents above her rounded ass.

She kept on her garters, her stockings and heels, even though this made her tower over me. I liked it. Liked running my hand up her thigh and feeling the patterned fishnets. Liked the quality of having her half-clothed rather than totally naked. It was sexier, somehow, and I knew that later, when she finally stripped, it would be exciting. A total reveal.

As if she could read my mind, Eleanor turned for me, so that I could kiss her braless breasts, tickle her nipples with the pointy tip of my tongue. But I realised, even as I lapped at her skin, that she wasn't a mind-reader. She was doing what felt good to her, as I was doing what felt good to me, licking and teasing my way down the front of her body until I reached the split between her legs. Once I was there, Eleanor laughed at me, at the look of awe on my face. On my knees in front of her, I lost in the wonder of her body, but as I brought my lips to her cunt and started to lap at her, I was exactly where I wanted to be.

After several moments, I had her sprawl out on the floor, so that I could have complete access, and then I went to work. Or play. Or heaven. She tasted like... like... Like I didn't know she would. Creamy, yes. Somewhat sweet. But heavier than I'd pictured. And sexier than I'd known. She was indescribable, and as I continued to lick and lap, her slippery juices made her thighs slick and wet.

With ease, I used my fingers to part her nether lips, holding her wide so that I could reach deep inside her. I wanted to climb in, to lose myself within the curves of her body. Eleanor wanted something else. She wanted to taste me, and she told me so as she moved my body, turning me so that my pussy was above her mouth and hers just below mine. We played each other, tricked and tickled, used fingers and tongues. There were circles and spirals and invisible designs. All the neat motions I've spent years describing. But the feelings were different. I wanted the night to be unending. Unlike my characters, I never wanted to come. I wanted this to last, and last. To spend the rest of my life in this position, head to tail with my lovely friend, keeping each other on that ridge without jumping.

Then, suddenly, I wanted something else. As Eleanor touched me and stroked me, the yearning changed, and I had to come. Desperate, just like any lover who has reached her peak. She came first, grinding against my mouth, raising her hips repeatedly off the floor and then slamming back down into the rug. And as she came, she moaned into my body, and I could feel her pleasure travel through me. This took me over, pushed me off, and I was falling. No words. No descriptions. Free-falling into a place I'd never been.

Not in reality. Not on paper.

You have to be careful when you search and replace. If you don't type the right command into the computer program, then as "he" becomes "her" all your "thes" become "thers". Replacing "him" in a word will change "shimmering" to "shermmering".

With Eleanor, I'd searched for words and replaced them instead with actions. Searched for fiction and found truth. And truth will beat out fiction every time.

The Game

Angela called that first party, almost two years ago, a trial by fire. Having to meet the entire band at one time. But, honestly, I preferred it that way, plunged into the group without a chance to step back, to move away from the flames.

Still, I was scared. I tried to control my nerves as I slid off her Harley, then waited while she set her gloves and helmet on the rack. We'd parked her bike in the circular driveway, already filled with other, more decadent bikes, and we walked past them to the front of the house.

"Guess we're the last one's here," Angel said, leading me up the stairs and into the Deleen DeMarco's Hollywood Hills estate. "That's good. You'll get to know everyone in about five seconds flat – then you can stop trembling and enjoy yourself." I nodded and gripped her hand. As a model, you'd think I'd be used to meeting celebrities – especially since I'm considered one myself. But I was fairly new on the scene. And meeting the members of Objects – the band with the most number one hits in the country – was disconcerting, regardless of how many fashion shoots I'd done.

Angel pulled me along behind her, whispering assurances to me: "You'll do fine. They'll love you." We brushed past the multi-coloured balloons that filled the entryway, lolling against he moulded doorways and fluttering softly up to the ceiling.

A poster of the new album cover, "Objects of Desire," was taped to one wall. It showed Angel, Deleen, Beauty, and Arianna totally nude with Keith Haring-style arrows pointing to their breasts and cunts. Lola, the cherub of the group with her blonde ringlets and innocent smile, sat naked in her wheelchair, staring up at the rest of the group.

As I looked at the picture, I realised how each band member derived power through individuality. Angel's tattoos were starkly severe in the black and white photo, as if they'd been carved into her body. Arianna had painted stars and stripes on her breasts to make them more patriotic. Deleen was like a mad sorceress. She winked at the camera with an almost evil smirk, and rubbed her hands together with glee. Beauty, who's half German and half Native American, had braided her thick, black hair into a solid rope – it made her look dangerous and mean. She stood sideways between Deleen and Arianna, and her braid hung down her back, past her shoulder-blades, almost to her waist.

"That's the uncensored version," Angel told me. "The public receives a model with black X's covering the indecent parts."

I stared, fascinated by the curves and dips of the women's bodies, their unique shapes, but Angel pulled on my hand, leading me into the sprawling living room. The lights were dimmed, and I almost stumbled over a white cat walking up to greet us.

"Hey, Shazzam," Angel picked up the kitty. "I'd like you to meet Katrina."

I shook a fuzzy paw, and Beauty, staked out on a matching sofa said, "Where are your manners, Angel?

You introduce your lady to a pussy before us?"

Angela shrugged, set Shazzam gently on the ground, and said, "Everyone, I'd like you to meet Katrina. Katrina, this is everyone." She looked around the room, "Well, almost everyone. Where are the hosts?"

Arianna, reclining on a matching red leather chaise-lounge with her girlfriend said, "Somewhere in the kitchen." She was covered by a petite Asian beauty named Sara, draped casually over her like a shawl.

"You should check out the spread," Beauty told us. "Tessa got the Sleeping Buddha to cater."

Angel and I turned as Tessa appeared in the doorway, caught beneath the iridescent light filtering through a gathering of balloons. Tess is a true Irish red-head, her ivory skin sprinkled with millions of freckles like golden confetti. They seemed to sparkle across her nose and shoulders and over her cleavage, and I wondered if they covered her entire body, then blushed at the thought.

Deleen came up behind her carrying a glass of champagne in each hand.

"Hey, Angel. Who's the babe?"

"Deleen, really," Tessa admonished. "You're frightening her."

"This is Katrina," Angela said, her arm behind me, pushing me toward them. I shook hands with Tessa. Deleen, passing the champagne on to Arianna and Sara, took one of my hands in both of hers and kissed my fingertips.

"Charmed," she smiled.

"Help yourself to food," Tessa said, ignoring her flirtatious lover, "We've got a feast spread out in the dining room, buffet style."

Angel and I piled up plates, then walked back into the main room and settled onto the floor against a flood of satin pillows. Tessa came to sit by my side. She had on a strapless dress with a black bodice and a short skirt of fluffy lace. Her slender waist was accentuated with a wide velvet ribbon. I complimented her on the look and she said, "Thanks. Easy on, easy off," and then leaned across me to ask Angel a question, rubbing her breasts slightly against my knees.

I wondered if she'd done it on purpose, and then looked at her startled as she asked me a question.

"I'm sorry, what?"

"Do you know Lola?"

"No. I know *of* her, but we haven't met."

"She should be here later," Tessa said, looking at Angel to include her in the conversation. "Lo was meeting with a publisher in New York about doing a book of photos. They say she's the next Herb Ritz." She paused, as an idea came to her, "You know, she ought to take some of you." Tessa said.

"The two of you together," Deleen interrupted. "Now, *that* would be a picture."

I saw Angel nodding in agreement, but turned when Arianna leaned up on the sofa, Sara moving with her lover's body as if she were another limb.

"Add Sara, too," Arianna insisted.

"And, um," Beauty fumbled as a gorgeous strawberry blonde strolled in from the kitchen holding a bottle of mineral water. She walked up to Beauty and snuggled against her.

"Liz," she purred.

"Yeah, and Liz," Beauty finished, lamely, and the rest of us laughed, transforming an awkward moment into a rather silly one. Liz didn't seem to mind. She curled her long limbs around Beauty's, protectively, like an owner.

"I wouldn't get too comfortable if I were her," Tessa

whispered to me. "Beauty left her last girlfriend on the plane when she met this one," Tessa nodded to Liz who was now kissing Beauty's earlobe. "Beauty's always had a problem with the word 'commitment'."

Angel excused herself, then, to get more food, and Tessa took this opportunity to lean even closer to me. Her body pressed against my side so that I could feel her fragile ribs, the warm, bare skin of her upper chest on my arm.

"How long have you two been hiding out?" she asked me when Angel was out of the room. "We haven't seem much of Angel since the recording ended."

"A month," I told her, thinking in my head that it was thirty days exactly since she'd come with Melanie to the fashion shoot at *Zebra*.

"And you met…"

"Through Melanie Samuel." I waited for the recognition to appear in Tessa's eyes.

"The journalist?"

I nodded.

"You're on the cover of *Zebra* this month, aren't you?" she said, getting it.

I nodded again, giving her a quick version of the smouldering look they'd had me do for the shoot – the one currently appearing on every newsstand. Lashes lowered, head tilted, lips pouting.

"You seem different in person," Tessa said, smiling at me. "So much younger."

"That's the makeup," I explained. "But it's what Angel said, too. It's what she liked about me, I think, the person beneath the image." Everyone in the business knows about it, but only a few people allow others into their shell.

Angel had said, "Can I talk with you?" And I told her,

knees trembling at the thought of talking with Angela McMorrow, lead singer in the hottest band in the country, "Hang out until I get this make up off." She'd waited, outside the dressing room, chatting with Melanie who kept yelling for me to hurry up. I came out in a T-shirt and ripped jeans, my normal attire, and Angela looked me over and shook her head.

"You're younger than all that, aren't you?" she asked, glancing toward the lights and the fancy dresses hanging from a metal pole in 'wardrobe.' "I'm the same age underneath" I grinned, "You just have to look beneath the surface."

Angel had nodded, moving in close to me as Melanie withdrew to answer her cell phone in private. "Yeah, I would like to do just that, Katrina. I would like to see what's lurking beneath your surface, peel you open, spread you out, learn each of your secrets for myself."

Then Melanie had returned and things continued as normal – at least until the next time Angel and I were alone. Still, I didn't say any of these things to Tessa. She would know all about duplicity, two-faced worlds, being the partner of Deleen DeMarco – someone whose little black book contained the number of every "in" person in Hollywood.

Angel came back then, now sitting on Tessa's side, and she gave me a look over Tessa's head that I took to mean, "How are you holding out?"

I shrugged back at her and then said, "Please," as Deleen stopped in front of me with a fresh bottle of champagne. It surprised me at first that there wasn't any 'help' at the party, but I was glad for it, glad for the low-key atmosphere. I could tell that these people were for real – not needing the constant stroking of fans or media.

The house – mansion, really – was as kickback as they

were – set up for comfort, not appearances, although all was stylishly done. There were pillows everywhere, velvet and satin striped, with butter-soft leather sofas. I hoped to decorate my own place in a similar fashion someday, wanting to be able to walk into a room, eyes closed (or blindfolded), and enjoy the surroundings by touch only.

By my third bubble-filled glass, I was leaning against the cushions, listening to Montage croon on the stereo, drifting in a warm fulfilment. I paid scant attention to Angel and Tessa who were discussing the promotion for 'Objects of Desire'. I watched as Arianna and Beauty gossiped across the space between their sofas, Sara describing her latest nude centrefold in *Planet X* magazine, and Liz, a first-class cabin attendant, explaining how Beauty had stolen her heart at 32,000 feet.

I wondered what had happened to the girl Beauty had been with, and I thought about asking Tessa, but she left to fetch a joint. When she returned to the living room, she was tottering on her spangled high heels.

"Want some, Angel?" she asked, collapsing on the pillows on Angel's left side, turning my lover into a "person sandwich" with Tess and me the bread.

"Naw, I'm saving my voice."

"Katrina?" she asked.

"Sure."

Marijuana goes to my head quickly, especially when I'm drinking, so I only took one hit. But Tessa apparently had been smoking in the bedroom before coming out. She was flying, and while I lit up, she leaned seductively against Angela and said, "You have the most beautiful eyes, Angel. You know it?"

Angel tried to brush her off, nicely, by saying,

"Deleen's the one with the killer eyes." Angel turned to me, "Did you know that Del's eyes have no colour?"

I was more stoned than I'd thought, because this statement tripped a string of bizarre images in my mind. "What do you mean?" I finally managed to ask.

"They're almost perfectly clear. She usually wears shades or coloured lenses to hide them. Del!"

Deleen looked over from her lazy-lioness position in the hammock chair.

"What's up?" She was gone, too.

"Come show Kat your eyes."

"Send the kitty over here."

I got up, also a bit unbalanced, and wove my way to Deleen's corner. She turned a floor lamp around so that the light shone directly in her eyes, and I drew in my breath. They were like glass, perfectly clear irises with liquid black pupils in the centre.

Deleen smiled at me and said, "I always wear contacts for public appearances. I wouldn't want to scare anyone."

She put his hand out to steady me. I'd been rocking in place, and her fingers were like flames licking at my skin. Startled, I stumbled back to the pillow corner. Tessa was now in Angel's lap, her dress hiked up to her thighs exposing the purple ribbons of her garters as she straddled my lover. Angel didn't seem uncomfortable, but I could tell she was humouring Tess.

"You don't mind, do you Katrina?" Tessa grinned at me. "Angel has the most inviting body. I wanted to be closer to it."

"Go ahead," I said magnanimously as I leaned against the wall, letting it support me as I slid to a sitting position. "Do what you have to." I wanted to see how far Angel would take it, wanted to know what I'd be in store for in the future. At the moment, she seemed to be letting

Tessa call the shots.

Deleen got up to open another bottle of champagne, and I saw a frown on her painted lips.

"What are you up to, Tess?" she asked, her buzz obviously worn off. Deleen's demeanour surprised me, considering how she'd flirted with me when we'd met.

"Just goin' for a ride," Tessa slurred, leaving no doubts that Angel was to be her horse.

Deleen clicked her tongue against the roof of her mouth, and then sat down on the nearest sofa, forcing Arianna and Sara to move aside. They protested for a second before resuming their positions: Sara had undone Arianna's leather jeans and was very quietly sucking on the strap-on dildo that Arianna wore in a harness. The darkness of the room had concealed their activity, but they didn't seem to mind being revealed. Arianna's moans and Sara's kitten-like suckling noises testified to that.

"What is it with you, Tessa?" Deleen's voice was very softly menacing. "It's been three hours since you last came, is that too long for you?"

Tessa looked at Deleen through clouded eyes. "I'm just entertaining our guests, Del," she said.

"Uh uh, baby, I'm not going to play that game." Deleen slid her hand through her silvery hair, apparently trying to calm herself down. Deleen's hair is completely grey and has been since her teens. She wears it combed off her forehead, and it falls like an old lion's mane straight down her back. "Get your little ass over here."

Tessa stood up quickly, a worried look replacing the lecherous one she'd worn only a second earlier.

"Now," Deleen ordered, when she saw Tessa hesitate.

Angel watched the whole scene with her features set. She appeared emotionless, a statue, but I could tell she was getting turned on. I was already able to read her expressions, the slight wrinkle in her brow or tightening of her jaw. I settled against her and she put an arm around me, gently turning my face to kiss my lips.

Tessa cautiously walked the rest of the way over to Deleen, as if condemned. As soon as Tess was in reaching distance, Deleen grabbed hold of her waist and threw Tessa over her lap. Tess struggled, realising suddenly what her Mistress meant to do, but Deleen held her firmly, scissoring one leg over Tessa's two squirming ones to keep her in place. Deleen lifted Tessa's dress by the hem, pulling it up to reveal a lavender lace G-string and matching garter belt.

"Katrina, would you mind bringing me my Harley gloves?" Deleen asked me, her voice unreadable except for the power in it, the command. "They're on the table in the entryway."

I looked at Angel to see if I should, but all she said was, "Go ahead, Kit-Kat, it's Del's party."

When I stood up, Deleen added, "Oh, and get me some K-Y, too, won't you? It's in the bathroom cabinet – the one in the hall." My heart racing, I left the room, gathered the tube of gel and the leather gloves, and walked back to Deleen who still held the upended Tessa over her knees.

"Thanks, sweetheart," Deleen said as I handed her the items. I turned to sit down next to my Mistress again, feeling weak and confused. Angel pulled me to her, positioning me between her legs so that I could feel the wetness that pulsed through her jeans.

Deleen slipped Tessa's G-string down her thighs, but left the garter and hose in place.

"Better calm down, Tess," her voice was hypnotic, and I realised suddenly that everyone in the room had turned to see what was going on. Sara and Arianna, after struggling into semi-upright positions, were watching intently. Liz and Beauty, who'd been up to something on their own plush sofa, were now mellowly regarding Tessa, Beauty softly explaining to Liz how Tess and Del's relationship worked. I heard Beauty say, "Don't worry, Lizzie, it's just how it is."

Deleen had her worn leather gloves on, and she squeezed a generous supply of the jelly onto one finger and then spread Tessa's ass cheeks with the other hand. Tessa continued to fight, but her slight frame was no match for Deleen's more powerful build.

"I said, 'Calm down,' Tessa."

Although Deleen hadn't raised her voice, there was a note of danger in it, one that made me sure that if I were in Tessa's position, I would be still. Tess must have sensed it, too, for she was suddenly quiet, yet I could tell her muscles were tensed to escape if Deleen would give her the chance.

"Tessa wants to come," Deleen said, addressing the rest of us as a group for the first time. "She has an insatiable appetite." As she spoke, she worked the K-Y around and into Tessa's asshole. When she slipped a gloved finger inside her naughty lover, Tessa started to protest again. Deleen put her lips close to Tessa's ear, but we all heard her hiss, "Once more, baby, and I'll get the studded gloves."

Now Deleen had two fingers inside her, and moved them in and out with increasing speed. She used her thumb on Tessa's clitoris, and Tess moaned, an obvious sound of pleasure that set off titters from Liz and Sara.

"Like that, don't you?" my Mistress whispered to me, and I nodded, leaning against her, feeling the hard synthetic cock that she was packing beneath the soft denim. Angel put both arms around me, protectively, as we continued to watch Deleen's progress with Tessa. Del was making her come slowly – bringing Tessa close to climax, then teasing her down. When she'd forced three fingers into Tessa's asshole, Tess started to move against her Mistress, fucking Deleen's gloved hand, working her body on it, but Del would have none of that.

"Tessa, don't," she said, a warning in her voice. It was obvious that Deleen did not want her lover to take any form of control, and I could tell that it took every ounce of Tessa's strength for her to follow this command.

"I'll make you come in my own sweet time," Deleen promised, before turning her attention to me. "Katrina? Tess was…" she cleared his throat before saying, "*riding* your property. Would you like to be the one to punish her?" She paused to look at me before continuing, "Because as soon as she comes, she's going to need to be disciplined."

The blood drained from my cheeks, and I turned immediately to Angel for help, but my Mistress shook her head, leaving the decision up to me, *testing* me, I thought. Flashes of conversations with Melanie replayed themselves in my head. "Leather," she'd said, "Bondage and Dominance. Sex Games. Wild, wild parties."

"I couldn't," I whispered.

"Another time," Deleen said, letting me off with a reassuring smile. Then, in a completely different voice, a darker voice, "Did you hear me, Tess? You'd better try to slow it down, because I'm going to spank your little bottom as soon as you come."

Tessa started crying, and I knew it was because she was close to orgasm. And that, humiliating though it might be to come in front of everyone, being spanked would be worse. Deleen continued finger-fucking her asshole and stroking her clit. I noticed how gently she stroked Tessa there, and understood that Beauty was right, that despite what Deleen had said, this was a game, with Tessa a willing player.

And then, with everyone's attention focused on her, Tessa flushed, closed her eyes tightly, and let her body finally respond to Deleen's attention. She arched her back, tense with concentration, and came in a series of powerful shivers, electricity running through her body.

The roomed seemed lit by her energy, a shower of metallic sparks, alien green and copper, vibrating in the air. She was truly stripped, as if Deleen had peeled her layer by layer, leaving a nude and shimmering soul for us to see.

How awesome it must feel to be that free.

Skin

Looking in the full-length mirror at Kitten's Top Drawer, I ran my fingers through my hair, and took a deep breath. My best friend was in the velvet-curtained dressing room next door to mine, and I stepped through the curtains and into her room. "I hate the way I look," I told Danielle. Yet it wasn't just that, was it? I'd changed recently, had started a new life. But my outside wasn't reflecting the new me.

Silently, I played with my long dark hair, holding up the curls so that the a few wispy strands fell loose on either side of my face, then twisting it in a familiar knot and tying it at the nape of my neck. Danielle gently pushed me aside so that she could see herself in the mirror.

"What you need is a change of attitude," she said, "I mean, that's why we're here, isn't it? New lingerie always helps to transform a mood."

"I don't know what to get," I told her.

Danielle didn't listen to my weak excuse, hurrying from the room in a pair six-inch heels as gracefully as if she were barefoot. What she brought back, the armloads of bras, panties, and garters, were accompanied by several Halloween costumes. Kitten's Top Drawer is known for lingerie, but in October they also carry both men and women's costumes.

"Here," she said, pushing a Little Red Riding Hood outfit into my hands and dragging me back into my dressing room. She left me with a pile of colourful lingerie and a serious look that said we weren't leaving until I'd tried on each piece.

I put on the costume first. It was perfect for me, and I hated it. Why did I always have to play the part of the innocent? I stuck my head into Danielle's dressing room again. Danielle had now zipped herself into a nurse's uniform that would have made for a perfect extra in a Benny Hill skit. With her curves, and the dress's naughty cut, it was difficult for me to think straight.

"Like it?" Danielle asked, grinning.

"I want the Harem Girl," I told her, referring to a costume I'd seen in the window.

"Don't we all?" she teased, but without waiting for my response, she went off in search of the saleswoman, not caring who saw her dressed as a naughty nurse. Danielle's like that. She treats the world as if it were a stage, and the people around her as if they are an audience. Wishing I could be more like her, I returned to my dressing room to try on the bra and panty sets. I was in a racy, candy apple red merry widow when Byron poked his head between the velvet curtains.

"Bingo," he said, "Ten points for me."

I stared at him as if he'd lost his mind.

"I mean, Christ, Lena. I recognised you by your feet. Aren't you impressed?"

I still didn't say anything. Was I supposed to be pleased that he'd found me?

"At first, I wasn't sure it was you," he admitted. "The red toenail polish put me off. You never do your toes. But I'd know the shape of your little piggies anywhere."

This was not the moment for me to run into my ex-boyfriend. First off, I was almost naked. Second off... actually, the naked part was the main reason. When you meet someone you used to sleep with, it is much more comfortable to be clad in a suit. Specifically, a suit of armour. Especially, when your ex- dumped you for another woman.

"What are *you* doing here?" Danielle asked. She had joined the conversation by parting the other velvet curtains, the ones that separated her room from mine. I instantly felt better at the sight of her. Now, instead of naughty nurse, she was dressed as a sexy witch, in a sheer black number with jagged edges that barely skimmed her luscious thighs. She looked like an erotic vision come to life, until you reached her expression – which sported the dictionary definition of the word "disdain". Her eyes burned cold when they looked at Byron, and if the costume had bestowed upon her any magical ability, I think she would have turned my ex-into a frog. Green, warty, and covered with a thin layer of slime.

"I've got a costume party at the law firm this year," he said, holding up the items he'd planned on trying. But before I could comment, Danielle lunged in.

"Gosh," my best friend said, scratching her chin, "Do they *have* a costume here for two-timing bastard? I didn't see one on the rack." Byron drew in his breath, but didn't respond, as if he were above Danielle's comment. But really, I knew, because he couldn't think of an equally snappy come-back.

"You look good," Byron said, tilting his head at me and completely ignoring my best friend. Danielle would have none of that. She doesn't like to be ignored – she prefers to do the ignoring herself.

"You were right," Danielle said to me as if Byron were no longer even there. "Jodi dumped him. Already. I owe you five dollars. I thought it would take a little longer for the ice princess to come to her senses."

Again, Byron did his best to rise above Danielle's comments, but this time he failed. His expression darkened, and rather than enter the next dressing room, he set the costumes on the floor and turned as if to leave. Then he stopped and came back, getting right up close to Danielle.

"I never liked you," Byron snarled. "I always thought you were a meddling cunt, and you are. You stick your nose into everything."

Danielle wasn't angry at all. This was her kind of fun. "You're right," she said smiling. "I stick my nose everywhere....And I mean, *everywhere*." She stretched the word out, using each syllable to let Byron know that she'd had her nose between my legs. Then she put her hands on her hips and waited, daring Byron to ask her exactly what that meant. I could tell from Danielle's stance that she was willing to go into excruciating detail.

Byron turned to look at me, and my cheeks must have turned the same crimson as the lingerie I had on. I knew that Byron now figured I'd been fucking Danielle all along, and I thought I should probably set him straight on the matter. But what did I owe him? Nothing. He glared at me for another second, and then turned away, this time really leaving the store.

Danielle watched him go, then tried to give me a high five, raising her open palm in the air. When I didn't bring mine up to meet it, she simply brought her hand back down to land on my ass, hard. My behind was hardly covered by the racy garment at all, and I jumped at the sting.

"Doesn't it feel good to know that he wants you, but he can't have you?"

I didn't answer. I couldn't decide how I felt at all. Seeing Byron hadn't made me want him. That wasn't it in the slightest. I pulled the curtains closed and stared at my reflection in the mirror. Taking a deep breath, I analysed the situation. Suddenly, I knew the feeling. It had made me want to leave that life behind. To really change myself and make the person reflected in the mirror match the one who lived inside the body. When I voiced this to Danielle, she swung the curtains closed around us, and said, "I know something that the 'old' Lena would never do."

I looked at her for a moment before understanding what she meant. Oh, God. She wanted to make love. Here. At our favourite lingerie store. I saw it in her pretty blue eyes, as clearly as if she'd spelled it out for me. And, you know what? I wanted to, as well. It didn't take any more convincing for me to let Danielle strip the merry widow off me, unhooking the tiny fastenings that ran up the back of the outfit. Then she forced me up against the mirror, and started to kiss me. Slowly, softly at first, just the slightest pressure of her lips against mine.

Sometimes kissing is better than anything else. The feel of it can send shivers all the way through my body. When you're in a long term relationship, you know the person you're with well enough to forgo kissing in favour of the other pleasures, which is sort of sad. But Danielle seemed to understand that she could spend minutes on my lips, licking, teasing, playing, and that would be enough for me. At least, for the beginning.

Her lips were sweet and soft on mine, and then they moved, slowly, down my neck. Here, Danielle forgot that she was supposed to be a witch, because she turned suddenly vampirish, biting me along my collar bones, nipping lower, so that I arched my body, offering myself to her. I could visualize what it would look like if she left teeth marks and lipstick-stained kisses all over me. And I liked the mental picture.

"Harder," I said, shocked at myself for making the request, but voicing it any way. "Bite me even harder, Danielle."

She gave me a slightly surprised look, but did as I asked, and the feel of her teeth against my skin had me dripping. My pussy was so wet that when Danielle cupped her hand over it, her fingers were instantly drenched in my liquid.

Danielle is friendly with the owners of the store, and no salesclerks interrupted us, offering more choices or telling us to stop doing what we were doing. We had the whole, large room to ourselves, and we made use of it, ultimately sprawling on the lush red carpet in a sixty-nine. Danielle kept her outfit on until the last possible minute, and that turned me on. Her naked body was only slightly hidden beneath the sheer, black fabric. I pulled it taut over her and stroked her through it, put my mouth against it and tasted her skin beneath the material.

Finally, when she could handle the barrier no longer, she pulled it over her head to reveal her nakedness. Her pale skin is almost startlingly white. No tan lines. No freckles. This time, I was the one to leave marks on her, biting at her thighs when she caused me so much pleasure that I thought I would scream. I spread Danielle's lips with my fingers and brought my tongue to her clit. Her juices were sweet, and I gripped onto her hips and pulled her cunt against my face. Wanting to drown myself in it. Danielle's pussy tasted slightly of the perfumed soap she used, combined with the fragrance of baby powder, a pale, talcum scent. Beneath it, she tasted of skin, of sin, of sexuality. She was delicious, and I sealed my lips to her font and drank as she did the same for me.

With pleasure, I lost myself in the curves of her body, in her taste, touch, and smell. As we brought each other to climax, I felt tears form in the corners of my eyes. It was so good. A shock, a surprise, the power of the orgasm slamming through me and leaving me weak and breathless, my body shaking. Minutes passed before I could regain the strength to sit up, to brush my hair out of my face and lick the last sweet drops of her juices from my lips.

Danielle sat up and watched me with a knowing look. Then, she moved to turn my face so that I was once again staring at my reflection. This time, when I gazed into the mirror I saw what I'd been hoping for – with my cheeks flushed and that hot, golden glow in my dark eyes, the transformation was complete. I looked like a different person outside. And that person finally matched the one who lives within my skin.

Hide

I have always loved the smell of leather, the feel of it on my skin. There is something insanely sexual about the texture, the way, after years of wear, it moulds to the owner's body. Perhaps it's the Neanderthal left in me, the cave girl clad in a mountain lion's hide, but wearing skins makes me feel more alive.

For myself, I choose sleek leather pants and riding boots, a leather vest worn open over a white T-shirt. On a lover, I like to see a black leather jacket cut close to the body, thigh-high leather boots pulled over opaque black stockings, and nothing, or very little, in between. I like to stroke a woman's skin through the skin, her hide through the hide, testing the dangerous "give" in the texture, the supple caress. Breathing in the sinful scent, the medley of near-intoxicating odours.

My love for leather has lasted close to 20 years, since I bought my first motorcycle and its accompanying biker jacket. And, despite a Harvard education and an inclination toward writing poetry, my fixation has become my means of employment: I own a leather goods store in the hip part of L.A., on Melrose Avenue.

At thirty-seven, I'm older than the kids who walk down the strip in racer-back tank tops and baggy jeans, younger than the matrons who glare as they drive by in their Jaguars and Saabs. About the same age as the woman who walked into my place in the middle of a slow day, a Wednesday afternoon.

She was stunning, just my type: long legs, red hair falling in loose curls past her shoulders, golden-green eyes that flashed at me in the late afternoon light. She strode into my store like a lioness on the prowl, the smell of her prey teasing her, making her fine nostrils flare as she moved up and down the aisles. I watched her from my perch behind the counter, watched as she touched the skimpy, pounded-leather dresses, ran her fingers along the smooth jackets, the shiny slacks.

I watched her, but I didn't say anything.

There are some customers who come in looking to buy clothes that will make them look cool. I recognise the posers, the Hollywood Rocker set, who belong to the young L.A. crowd. They're happening only because they're young and in L.A. These jokers snag the vinyl jeans, the butt-hugging suede, the thigh-high micro minis. Others, my raunchy sex-fiends, buy shiny black chaps, cut-away dresses, unbelievably short shorts, bras and bikinis studded with silver. They spare no expense to buy what it takes to make them come, and I cull most of my money from them.

But I wait for, and wish for, and fantasize about the she-tigers, the lady lions, the ones, like this redhead, who need the feel of the hide on their naked skin. Need the scent of it caressing their lovely bodies. These customers are the ones I opened 'Hide' for in the first place, and they are the beauties I wait for.

And watch.

She had on a mint-green halter top that made her eyes glow the same colour, and cut-off jeans that showed me a bit of her panties when she bent to look at the boots lined on the wall. Her ass made me dizzy, the way it filled out those shorts, the way the faded denim hugged her sweet tail. She was a beauty, a thoroughbred. A prize.

"Do you have this in a sex?" she asked softly, startling me from my daydreams of what she'd look like in a black leather jacket, fishnets, and black motorcycle boots. Startling me from a picture of her tied down to my bed with all leather gear in place and a pair of stiff scissors in my hand.

"A *six*?" she repeated, moving closer to the counter. I saw that look in her eyes, the look of the huntress, the look of the goddess, and I nodded, quickly, and motioned for her to follow me to the back.

She did, high-heeled sandals clicking on the wood floor, and I opened the door and ushered her in, spreading my arms to show her my private collection.

"Ohhh." A sigh. She had found Nirvana.

"Your size," I said huskily, "Everything. All of it. Try on any piece you want." She went quickly to the first rack, her long red nails stroking the sides of the lace-up pants, her palms caressing the velvety-soft insides of the jackets. Butter-soft leather, black as midnight, some pieces shiny, others worn with age and love.

"Where?" she asked, looking around the room. There are mirrors on the walls, but no private dressing room in the back.

"You can use the rooms out front," I told her. "Or change right here."

She shot me a look, one that made me melt. "Here's fine."

In a second, her green top was on the floor, her shorts next, and panties last – no bra, she didn't need one – and she was into the first outfit before I could fully register the concept of her body. The skin, the hide, sliding against her pale, naked body, turned me on more than anything I can possibly imagine, more than simply staring at her nude form could have done. She'd chosen one of my favourites, right from the beginning, a pair of tight black riding pants and a matching vest, worn over nothing but her pale, creamy skin. She slid into her sandals then swung her hair out of the way to catch her reflection in the mirror.

"That was made for you," I mumbled.

She nodded, more to her mirror image than to my statement, and stared at herself in the critical way that I've noticed even very pretty women do. That look never appears on my own face. I'm secure in my body, in the strength of it, the lines of it, but that may be because of my years or may be because my father treated both his daughters and sons alike. We were given no special treatment, no coddling. When I look in the mirror I don't see a painted picture, a gilded reflection. I see straight to my soul.

She wasn't sure, wasn't totally satisfied, and she kicked off the shoes, peeled down the slacks and went rifling through the racks, clad only in the leather top, showing me all of her charms, her golden-furred pussy when she turned my way, her pink pussy lips when she bent over.

"Do you like that?" I asked as she reached for a dress, one with laces at the sides and back. It was a dress made for a motorcycle-lady, made as specifically for this woman as if she had been the designer's muse.

She slipped off the vest for an answer, sliding the dress over her head and then stalking toward me and turning, wanting me to fasten the laces in back. I did it with shaking hands, moving her long hair out of the way so that I could do it right. She was tall, at least 5'10" in bare feet, and the dress fitted her like a leather glove. She moved away as soon as I was done with the laces, sidling up to the mirror and then pirouetting in front of it.

She liked this one better. I could tell. The way she pursed her lips at her image, the way she moved a few feet back and looked down, her chin tilted at an angle, taking in her entire reflected twin.

"You could try it with fringe boots," I suggested, unsure of how much input she wanted. She seemed to be on a mission, and if she were buying to please a lover, I'd have to watch my step.

"Yeah," she looked at me expectantly. "What do you have?"

I rushed to get the highest pair from the rack out front and grabbed my favourite motorcycle boots, as well. While I was nearby, I shut and locked the front door, turning the "Out to Lunch," sign face forward.

When I returned, she was still standing in front of the mirror, but now she had on a pair of fishnet hose, snagged from one of the inventory boxes. "Hope it's okay," she said, giving me a different kind of look with those lake-green eyes.

"Sure." *Anything you want,* unsaid, but implied. I handed over the boots and she slid them on. Again, a perfect fit. She walked a few steps forward and a few steps back, almost doing a dance. Then she turned to face me.

"What do you think?"

Did she want a salesperson's opinion, or one of a lust-filled admirer?

"You're stunning," I said, my husky baritone going down another octave. But I was quick to correct myself, my mind working instantly, "I mean, it looks stunning on you." I've never been one to stutter. As I said, I have always felt confident with my dark looks, confident in the lean, sturdy weight of my body, but this woman made me shake.

"Yes," she turned to regard the mirror again. "I like this one best."

I pulled together my nerve. "Is it for a special occasion?"

"No. Just for myself. I needed a lift. And leather always makes me feel... sexy. Something about the scent, the smell of it."

I nodded.

"You understand," she asked, "Don't you?"

"It's why I have the store," I told her, wanting to touch her, restraining myself from taking her in my arms and stroking her through the soft leather, feeling the place, the wondrous place where her skin ended and the hide began. The leather and the skin, the hide on the hide. Circling it, sniffing it, getting down on the floor and pressing my face to her body, wrapping my arms and around her waist and smelling *her* animal scent through the musky odour of the hide.

"What's your name?" she asked then, breaking me from my daydreams.

"Patrice." My voice sounded so deep to my own ears. Deep and filled with longing. I wanted to own her.

"I'm Diana."

Of course she was. Diana, goddess of the moon. The queen and the huntress.

She walked a step closer, clicking in those fringed boots. "Why do you keep all of the best back here?"

The honest reason is that I don't want it to appear on just anyone. You need to love leather to wear it right. I've only found a few people I considered worthy of owning the best. This lady was definitely one of them.

119

"I don't like to waste it."

Now she was the one to nod. Another step closer. "Patrice?"

"Yeah."

"Do you want to feel?"

Another step.

I bowed my head. *Was she teasing me?* "Yeah."

She moved quickly then, into my arms, and I rested my head on her shoulder and breathed in the smell of her body, right at the underside of her neck, that secret, haunting she-woman-smell. Then, with her scent still tickling my nose, I went down to my knees and pressed my lips to her sex, kissing her here, smelling her here, getting wave upon wave of the mingling perfumes, the leather and the lady, the sweet smell of the old leather, the fresh scent of the woman.

I stroked her body through the skin, dragging my palms firmly along the sleek lines of her hips, over her thighs. She moved away from me, dancing away, sliding free from the dress and returning to the rack, completely nude, choosing another pair of pants and a tight jacket with zippered sleeves. She never took her eyes off me as she pulled on the pants, wriggled into the jacket. She zipped into the second pair of boots, the cycle ones. Then she came back, wanting me to feel her again.

I grabbed her lower this time, moving my hands down her calves to her ankles. Holding her tightly here, through two layers of leather, the slacks and the boots. Gripping into her body firmly enough so that she could feel my strength. My desire. In my mind, I could hear a poem (hundreds of years old), that could have been written for her specifically. A poem for a huntress:

Lay thy bow of pearl apart.
And thy crystal-shining quiver;

Give unto the flying heart
Space to breathe, how short soever
Thou that mak'st a day of night,
Goddess excellently bright.

I suddenly knew what it would be like to have her riding behind me on my Harley, her arms tight around my own waist. Knew what it would be like to reach our destination, up at the top of the Hollywood hills in a secret grove of eucalyptus trees, where we'd be alone except for the moon and the wind. I'd turn her around, bend her over the seat, and slide those leather jeans over her hips and *down*.

"Down," she said, again pulling me out of my fantasies. "Lie down."

I followed her order immediately, going quickly from my knees to my back on the wooden floor, watching wide-eyed as she straddled my legs and slid down my thighs until she was sitting sex-to-sex on top of me.

She could tell that I was packing, I was sure of it, the synthetic cock pressing at her through two pairs of leather jeans. She could feel the ache of it, wanting her, and she smiled as she reached out and stroked it, stroked *me* through the hide, caressing me. I could tell from her look of ecstasy that I had met my match. Finally, after many years of searching, many more laying in wait, I had found my leather lady.

She didn't touch the button fly, didn't make any move to undo my pants, she only stroked, and teased, and played with me through the worn leather.

But she denied me.

Her hands continued to work, her fingers to dance their intricate steps up and down the crotch of the jeans. Then, without saying a word, she began moving her body

121

forward, taking over from her fingers with her sweet little pussy, rubbing in circles, endless circles of her hips against mine. Around and around. I helped her, grabbing onto her waist and finding that fast, pounding beat. Moving her up and down, then a quick circle, up and down the rigid shaft of the moulded cock. Wanting nothing more than to rip open the buttons, tear off her slacks, and slam it into her. But then, wanting nothing less than losing the feel of the leather, the softness of it, the slender caress of it tight on us both.

"Want do you want?" I managed to whisper, the image of her on my cycle still burning in my head, the feel of her skin where it showed, at her wrists, at the neck of her jacket, at her throat, the bits that I saw inflaming me. The leather of her body, the hide and the hide, engulfing me.

"What do you want?"

If she needed me inside her, I would. I would take down her slacks, unbutton my own, and plunge the phallus into the wet heat of her pussy. I could smell that wet heat, knew what it would feel like as it dripped down the plastic dildo and matted against my fur. But if she wanted to come in the leather, come *through* the leather, I'd do that too.

She surprised me.

"Sh, Patrice. Don't say anything. Let me."

In a flash, she was up and grabbing the motorcycle gloves from the edge of my desk. Then she motioned for me to stand and undo my fly. I did it, my fingers slipping only once in their hurry to loosen the buttons.

Her gloved hand reached in, took over, freeing the flesh-coloured cock and bringing it to her lips. The leather-covered fingertips reached lower, probing, trying to find my cunt beneath the harness. I didn't need her to touch me there, simply watching her mouth around the head of the cock, drove me crazy. She worked me hard, worked me well, sliding the cool leather across the feverish skin of my flat belly, bringing me to a boiling point with the inferno of her mouth as she deep throated the cock and pressed her lips all the way to my body. She knew... she knew everything. The two sensations, skin on skin. The slickness of her glossy lips, then the smooth leather caress, the heat of her tongue trailing lower to tickle my thighs, then the heavy weight of her gloved going back between my legs to tickle my asshole.

I stroked her fiery curls while she worked, faster and faster, the glove and her tongue, the leather sliding on the wetness of the cock, the oiled-up feeling as her hand moved piston-fast on the shaft. But then suddenly, she settled back on her heels and looked up at me with a mixed expression of lust... and anticipation. I did not let her down.

I drew her to her feet, lifted her into my arms, and brought her to my heavy wooden desk. Quickly, I peeled the gloves from her hands and slid them on my own, delighting in the warmth left by her body heat. Then, just as quickly, I unzipped her leather slacks and pulled them down, only to her thighs, giving me the perfect access to her pussy and asshole. Lovely. Perfect. I parted her ginger-furred kitty lips with two fingers and found her clit, teasing it with my gloved hand. Brushing my fingertips against it until she cried out from the intensity.

Then I went to work with my mouth, treating her as she had treated me. My fingers and my tongue. The leather and the love. I could not get enough, tickling her with my thumb and forefinger until her juices ran down the sweet silken slit between her thighs. Then I lapped every drop, breathing in deeply to catch the most haunting woman-smell, musky and sublime, mixed with the scent of the leather, warm, dark. Living.

The combination of it: the smell of her, the taste of her, the mingling scents together had my pussy dripping sweet juices down my thighs. Before she could come, I stood, grabbing her around the waist, and impaled her with the cock, slamming into her, pressing my body hard against hers. Poetry in motion, this time written by yours truly.

Sinful. Dangerous. Wild. Alive.
The skin on the skin. The hide on the hide.

Above You

Josh and I find each other at a convention. He likes me from the start because I pay no attention to him. None at all. I don't notice him when I walk by his booth. I don't make eye contact with him from my stool in the dimly lit hotel bar. I am not playing favourites. I never pay attention to potential bedmates at the trade shows. Not because there aren't any attractive possibilities, but because I have zero desire to hook up for three days with some total stranger and then spend the next ten years at these conventions in a practised study of avoidance.

But Josh is different.

He searches me out, and he tells me things that men in L.A. don't bother saying. At least, not to me. He says that I'm unlike anyone he knows (in Erie, Pennsylvania). With his arm around my waist and his head bent low to my ear, he whispers that I've got a quality, a mystery, an aura. From the moment he saw me, arranging the books in our booth, he knew he had to meet me.

"You're different," he says, and the pull of his accent makes him suddenly sexy. "I don't know anyone like you."

It's as if he's never seen a girl with dyed black hair before. Never seen pale skin or dark eyes, all of the things that make me an aberration in Hollywood where blonde and blue are the only colours in the crayon box. But I've seen people like Josh before. Tall, lean, and handsome in a hick sort of way. He's probably very suave (in Erie, Pennsylvania), but a little bit more earnest than the type I go for. Read between the lines: I'm just like Josh. I yearn for the ones who ignore me.

Josh says that he loves me.

And he says it even before I go down on him in the elevator.

When I meet Josh's girlfriend at the trade show the following spring, I'm surprised by how much we look alike. We are both petite, fair-skinned brunettes. I've got an inch or two on her and she's got about ten pounds on me. As we size each other up, I believe we come to the exact same conclusion: I am slightly prettier, a bit hipper, and much happier than Sarah is. The first two items on the list could be taken care of in a single afternoon. What she needs most is a good haircut and a much better dress. She could use a tattoo, or a hidden piercing, something to make her feel funky and confident that the rest of the world doesn't know about. The happier aspect is more difficult to work with. I think that it's got nothing to do with me and everything to do with Josh.

Winning at the attractiveness game gives me an odd upper hand. An air of queendom, like when you're five years old and it's your birthday party and you get to boss other people around all day long. Sure, it's fun, but after everyone leaves, you feel sort of sick to your stomach.

As if she enjoys wallowing, Sarah befriends me. She drinks too much and puts her head on my shoulder. I feel her soft hair against her neck, her breath on my cheek when she speaks. "You're so nice," she slurs, "that's what Josh told me."

I wonder what else he told her. I've had crushes before, have gone loopy and started confessing unusual factoids about a person I liked to the one I was currently with. Did Josh talk that way about me? Or did he describe the way it felt to press me up against the elevator door, to ride me as the car travelled all the way up to the thirty-second floor?

My obvious queenliness draws other men to me while Sarah is ignored. The scruffy musician at the bar dedicates his set to the raven-haired beauty, and he nods in my direction. The waiter at our table brings me a round of free drinks. And then, of course, there's Josh.

Josh. Josh. Josh.

His foot meets mine under the table. His fingertips linger when he hands me a fresh drink. Long glances over Sarah's head make me feel as if he's not only mentally undressing me, but mentally bending me over the shaky table and fucking me doggy-style. Poor Sarah pretends that everything is normal, and I do my best to pretend along with her. Until I get too drunk to care.

Josh's brother lives in town, and when we meet him late in the evening at a club, an even more bizarre scene is waiting to unfold. Mark and Josh have their own competition going on, and when Mark sees that Josh likes me… then Mark likes me. And then suddenly it's Mark. Mark. Mark.

Mark is married with a two-year-old daughter named Lucy. He isn't as handsome as Josh, but he's cooler in a nerdy, Buddy Holly sort of way. He knows stuff about music, and he's not just feeding me a line when he says that he's into hip-hop. He really is. We stay at the club in Baltimore until two in the morning and I dance the whole set with Mark. No cabs come to pick us up and we end up walking nearly two miles back to the hotel. Mark walks next to me, and Josh insists on walking right behind us, listening in on our conversation. Mark torments his younger brother, asking me sexy questions, making Josh jealous. And because Josh's jealous, I sense that Sarah wants to crawl into a hole in the sidewalk and die.

"I'll bet you're not wearing any panties," Mark says, just loud enough for Josh and Sarah to hear. I don't answer because I don't have to. Three sex-hungry people are now picturing me without panties. It doesn't matter whether I have them on or not. To Mark and Josh and Sarah, I am totally naked beneath my skirt. But I'm picturing Sarah's panties. I know she's wearing them, and I'm sure that they are plain, white, and cotton.

At the hotel, Mark offers to come upstairs with me while Josh leads an extremely intoxicated Sarah back to her room. She shoots me a look over her shoulder that I read as 'I won.' Her drunken smile is lopsided and she winks.

"Be right back," Josh says. "Just going to tuck her in."

He does it, I know, because deep down he loves her. Not me. I am a fantasy creature flown in from L.A. to solve his problems and star in his daydreams. She is the woman he ought to be with.

"And I'll tuck *you* in," Mark says with a sly smile.

"You're married."

"That's my problem."

"Mine, too," I say and leave him before he can grab me and hold me back. I don't want him. I want Josh, and even though I shouldn't be, I'm surprised when he doesn't come to my room, when he doesn't even ring after putting Sarah to bed. That is, at first, I'm surprised. Then I get mad. Finally, I get an idea. Although not as drunk as the rest of them, I feel my liquor as I reach for the phone. No answer at Josh's room, so I try Sarah's, not sure how I'm going to behave as she answers the phone. Turns out I don't have to worry about anything. She says simply, "I was about to call you. Come on over."

"Over" means up two floors to her room. Maybe she wants to talk. To ask me questions. To dish Josh. I don't feel like being alone, so I grab my key and ride the elevator to her floor, thinking of my ride with Josh six months earlier.

Sarah opens the door naked. I see her clothes in a mess on the floor by the bed and realise that I was wrong. Not plain white underwear, but a pair of racy black panties. High-cut on the hips. Panties I'd wear myself. Slowly, I start to reconsider the situation.

"I was just having a drink," Sarah says, shutting the door behind me and then walking across the room toward the balcony. Her haughty ass is a pleasure to watch, and I stare openly, considering my next move. I still feel the alcohol buzzing through my system, but that simply makes it easier for me to get naked myself and walk after her. It seems only fair for us to be at the same starting point. But even when I'm without clothes, I sense that she's leading. Our roles of the evening have changed. This is her game.

Sarah hoists herself up so that she's sitting on the cold concrete wall that rims the tiny area. That makes me nervous, but she doesn't seem frightened at all. Behind her, the sky begins to lighten, still a deep blue, but no longer cobalt. Toward the east it gradually turns a faded denim colour, like worn jeans.

"Look at me," Sarah says softly, bringing my attention from the sky back to her face. I see suddenly that she's very pretty. That she is different from me; it's only the surface parts that are similar.

"Do you love him?" Sarah asks.

I shrug and shake my head at the same time, spending several moments drinking in her features. She has freckles, which I hadn't noticed before. In the lights from the city, her skin takes on a golden glow, as if she'd been covered with sparkling confetti.

"Did you do it?" she asks next.

"What?" I murmur.

"Fuck. Did you fuck?"

It sounds harsh coming from her lips, and I squint at the way she says the word, then nod.

"Would you fuck me?"

I realise that I misread her cues all evening long. Sarah wasn't playing the part of the left-out girlfriend, she was flirting with me. Her head on my shoulder. Her sweet compliments. The dirty looks she shot Josh whenever he made a forward move. While I was concocting a soap opera cat fight over a guy, Sarah was letting me know that I'd turned her on. Thoughts of Josh slip away. Now, I want to play connect the dots of Sarah's freckles with my tongue, start at a freckle on her chin and work down her neck, over her breasts, along the flat of her belly, to her cunt. I also don't want her to fall off the railing, so I pull her down and then spin her around, so that she can look out at the slowly waking city while I work.

Of course, it isn't really work. The feel of her soft skin under my fingertips, under my tongue, is the ultimate pleasure. I lean up against her, so that she can feel my skin on hers, and then I press my lips to the back of her neck and lick her, then bite her. She shivers against me, and makes a soft sighing noise to let me know she likes it.

Different lovers bring out different sides of your

130

personality. Somewhere deep inside me, I know this. Josh put me in the role of the lady, a damsel, but it takes making love to Sarah to remind me that I have a range of facets. That I can be passive with one lover and dominant with another. And I am dominant with Sarah. I play her, sliding my hands up her arms, locking her wrists together in one hand as I bend to bite the nape of her neck the way a mama cat does when it lifts a kitten. Sarah coos and I bite harder, now releasing her wrists and using one hand to spank her ass.

The pre-dawn air flows over our naked skin, and this makes it even more spectacular as I work my way down her body, licking along the ridge of her spine, until I find the indents above her bottom. I kiss her here, waiting, forcing myself to take my time until she arches her back. Letting me know with that single move what she wants. And what she wants is exactly what I want. My tongue in her asshole. The warmth of it, the length of it. Pressing in and pulling out while she grips onto the concrete barrier and faces into the morning sky, as still as one of the gargoyles on the roof above us.

I do just as we both hoped I would, parting the cheeks of her ass, introducing her to the wetness of my tongue. I trick it in a circle around her hole before plunging inside. She makes that cooing noise again, like one of the doves on the window ledges in the room next to us. I adore that noise, want to hear it again, and I continue with my actions. Feeling her inside with my tongue, bringing one hand up the split of her body in front and tweaking her clit between my fingers. I want to make her scream, want to take her to places she'd only been in her mind.

As the sky continues to lighten, I work her, fucking her with my tongue and fingers. When I sense that she's close to coming, I withdraw my tongue and turn her around, letting her feel the cold wall behind her while I spread her pussy lips and made love to her clit. Anyone can eat pussy, but it takes a truly special lover to focus. To do the things to your partner that you'd most like someone to do to you. I do everything to Sarah that I like the best. I take my time, which is always important, and I bring her repeatedly to the edge of climax without letting her reach it.

You never want your lover to get there too soon. Yes, it will feel good. Nobody has ever had a "bad" orgasm. But the best ones are those that you can almost taste in your mouth before they wash through your body. This is the kind I bring to Sarah, finally sealing my mouth to her cunt and letting my tongue flick over and over her clit. Repeatedly. Varying the intensity until she grips onto my shoulders and screams. The contractions rage through her, slamming through her body and leaving her both satisfied and drained, staring down at me with a look of total satisfaction in her lovely eyes. I don't have to ask her how it was, and she doesn't have to tell me. But she whispers one word, "Perfect," and smiles.

In the morning, I stop by Josh's hotel room to say goodbye.

"I love you," Josh says softly. This time, there's no oral sex involved. Just Josh, looking almost tearful as he stares at me from the rumpled mess of his white bed sheets. "I love you."

And that's the last I ever hear of him.

"Maybe he didn't say that," Sarah suggests when I tell her the story afterward on our flight to L.A.

"What do you mean?" I ask, looking over at my new girlfriend. She couldn't be more different from Josh. She talks straight, doesn't play games, and would never let a lover come between her and her brother.

"Maybe you misheard him."

"Love… shove… dove…"

"Above," she says with finality. "Maybe he said, 'I'm above you,'" she pauses, considering the situation. "Was he?"

"Was he what?"

"Above you?"

I picture Josh's long lean body sprawled among the wrinkled white sheets. In my head, I can still hear him whispering the words. "I love you." That's what he said. No doubt about it. But that statement becomes our private joke for ever. When Sarah wants to kiss me, to touch me, to fuck me, she leans in close and says, "I'm above you."

She's not. We are on the exact same level.

Which, I might add, is way the fuck above Josh.

Wanna Buy A Bike?

In Amsterdam, you can prove the Rolling Stones wrong. Here, you actually *can* always get what you want. That is, if what you want are drugs – any drugs – or sex – any sex. Sex with men. With women. Orgies. S/M. B/d. Name the perversion and you can make it come true.

Sure, I understand the benefits of having such readily available pleasures. In the States, you have to search out the seedier sides if you've got a taste for trouble. So I realise how someone might enjoy being able to walk down an alley, point to a window, and buy the person behind it for an hour of frisky fun. Yet the type of free-wheeling environment found in Amsterdam poses a problem for girls like me. Girls who like the darker side of things.

The rush, I've always found, is in delving into that cloak and dagger ambience and plunging down the steps into the unknown. What's illegal in Amsterdam? You can walk into a coffee shop and buy your marijuana, walk into a pharmacy and purchase magic mushrooms. No need to skulk through alleys after your personal yearning. For some, it's a fantasy come true. But I fucking hate it.

This is why I was sulking miserably through a rainy Amsterdam afternoon, a scowl on my face, my long black hair windswept, my eyes troubled. In each cosy cafe, college students sent fragrant plumes of smoke toward the lazily spiralling ceiling fans. Content and flush-cheeked, the smokers slipped deeper into their daydreams, looking as if they were right out of a painting – Norman Rockwell for the new millennium.

In the red light district, I knew I could find someone to take care of whatever I craved, which made me crave absolutely nothing. While others tightened their coats against the harsh, autumn storm, I rebelled in the only way I could, pushing back the hood of my heavy black jacket, pulling open the buttons, letting the water hit my skin.

The one thing I do love about Amsterdam is the set-up of the city, intricate circles and circuits of canals. Wet and pungent, filled with houseboats, fallen leaves from gold-flocked trees, ducks, and debris. I like the idea of the circles, one slipping inside of the other as they get closer to the centre. Rings around rings, like the spiralling efforts of a lover's tongue nearing the bull's eye of a woman's clit.

With thoughts like that on my mind, it was no wonder that I was aroused. But I felt as if I were on the verge of coming without ever being able to reach the climax. Searching for something unknown in a city where you can get anything as long as it has a name and you have the price –

"Wanna buy a bike?" a voice asked as I rounded a corner, breaking through my unhappy haze. Turning, I saw the first evidence of the Amsterdam underground. A scruffy looking youth, with tousled birch-coloured hair and a dead-eyed green stare captured my attention. Handsome, but weathered about the edges, he had the look of someone who'd been up all night. It's a look that I find seductive.

"Excuse me?" I asked.

"Pretty girl," he beckoned, and I took a step further away from the crowds of tourists and into the mouth of the stone-cobbled alley where he stood. "Do you wanna buy a bike?"

And now I understood. Where, in any other city, this man would be offering me drugs or sex or something not easily found on the street, he was hawking bicycles instead. Good as gold in Amsterdam.

"Cheap," he added in perfect English. "With a seat and handlebars. Everything."

In Amsterdam, you have your choice of how to get around. You can walk – like I do – use a trolley, a boat, a car (if you have balls of steel), or a bicycle. The problem, in my opinion, is that everyone is stoned on something, and they drive as if to prove that you can handle a vehicle while your mind is flying. Trolleys split pedestrians and make them scurry for safety. Bicycles cut off cars. I might trust myself on two wheels, but I wouldn't trust those around me. Still, the excitement of embarking upon something illicit made me shift in my wet jeans. Danger is my all-time favourite aphrodisiac.

"Where is it?" I asked, looking around.

"Don't carry the product on me," he said tersely, and I thought I saw a sneer on his attractive face, as if he was thinking, 'What can you expect from a foreigner?'

"How much?"

He leaned forward to quote the price, and I saw the way his eyes looked at me. As if he'd suddenly noticed that my jacket was open, my lipstick red T-shirt wet and tight on my slim body. My jeans soaked through.

The price he quoted was high for a bicycle, but low to fulfil my need. I nodded, and he motioned for me to follow him, back down that alley to another. Quick-stepping as we made our way to some unknown destination, I heard the way my boots sounded on the walkway, that staccato beat, heard the echo of my beating heart in my ears. This was adventure, excitement, the reason I'd come to Amsterdam in the first place. And why was I getting all warm and aroused? Silly girl, silly girl. It was because I was about to buy a bike.

"This way," he urged, "just down that street."

I tried to keep up with him, but ended up walking behind, and that was okay. The rear view of this youthful dealer was something to be admired. Like me, he had no qualms about getting wet, and his Levi's were a dark ocean blue, tight on his fine ass, slicked down on his lean legs. He had on a black sweater, also drenched, and that unruly white-blond hair that seemed bed-rumpled instead of just plain wet.

When we got to our destination, he wanted the money. But I've made deals with street salesmen before. It's important to see the merchandise before you put up the cash, regardless of the country you're in.

"Don't trust me?" he asked grinning, and I shook my head. "This way, then," he said, and we continued on our route, around one of the comeliest canals of the city, where even the ducks were now hiding beneath the arched bridges to stay away from the cold, driving rain. What did they have to worry about? They lived in water.

"Just a bit further," he said, and I wondered as I spotted a familiar-looking kiosk whether we were going in circles. Didn't matter to me. I'd have followed as long as he led. But soon he stopped again, this time in front of one of the skinny gingerbread-coloured houses that tour-leaders love to point out as the "charm" of Amsterdam. Chained to a railing was a shiny blue bicycle, just as he'd described. Two wheels. Handlebars. A seat. Everything.

"You believe me now?" he asked, and he took a step closer as he held out his hand for the money. His fingertips could have brushed my breasts through the tight, damp shirt, could have stroked the line of my chin, tilted my head up for a kiss. I felt my breath speed up, but I didn't let on. I can play as streetwise as I need.

"The key?" I asked, pointing to the bike lock, and the corners of his eyes crinkled at me as he smiled again. He seemed to have more respect for me now, sensed that I was willing to play any game he named.

"A little further," he said softly, turning on his heel and continuing the walk. Such a smart-ass, I thought. He'd have taken my money at the first place, then told me to wait while he got the bike, disappearing for ever. At the second stop, where I could actually see *a* bike, he would have made more excuses – "I need to get the key" – and then vanished. Now, we were testing each other. Him to see if he could get the money from me. And me to see if he might sense something else that I wanted.

Once again, we were back down another alley. At the end, stood a long metal rack, with at least fifty cycles attached. The dealer nodded toward the mess of cycles. "You choose one," he said, "tell me the colour, and I'll get it for you. *Then* you pay."

"I'll need a lock, too," I said.

"Locks are no good. Watch what I do to one."

I looked over the rack of bikes and found one that I liked. "The emerald green."

He smiled. "Five minutes. Meet me back there," and he pointed down the alley to a bridge. "On the other side."

This was fine with me. If he didn't show up, I wasn't out anything. If he did, well, we'd just see. For the first time, I felt happy to be in Amsterdam. The city *was* lovely, even rain-streaked, and the abundance of drugs and easy sex made the people around me seem at peace. Who isn't blissful when they've just gotten laid, or smoked a big fat one, or done both simultaneously?

At the meeting spot, I waited in the rain, shivering, and in less than five minutes, he was there, wheeling the bike ahead of him. Now, it was my turn to pull a fast one.

"I have to get the money," I said. His eyebrows went up and he frowned at me, but I shook my head quickly to reassure him. "I have it, but it's at my hotel," I told him, naming the location. My smile must have let him know what I was offering. More than payment for a bike. "Don't you trust me?"

"We'll ride there," he said, "it's quicker."

I found myself perched on the back wheel as we sped down the streets, cutting off taxis and trolleys, wreaking havoc with pedestrians, and then joining a sea of other cyclists until finally we were at my hotel. He carried the bike into the lobby for me, where the concierge promised to watch it. Then we headed up the stairs together, soaking wet, dripping little puddles on the carpet as we walked.

At my room, I paid him first, just in case that was really all he wanted. He took the money, folded it, and slid the bills into the side pocket of his jeans, just before he slid his jeans down his legs. Smiling, I stripped, as well, and soon we were naked together, pressed against the wall of my hotel room. Our bodies were wet and cold, at first, then wet and a little warmer as we created heat together.

I like sex. Especially unexpected sex. And this beautiful boy seemed perfectly ready to give me what I needed. He took his time. Starting with a kiss, he parted my lips with his, met my tongue, moving slowly, carefully. Then he grabbed both of my wrists in one hand and held my arms over my head, pinning me to the wall. With my wrists captured, he brought his mouth along the under-curve of my neck, then kissed in a silky line to my breasts. I arched my back, speaking to him with my body alone, making silent, urgent requests. He didn't fail me. First, he kissed my left nipple, then my right, then moved back and forth between them until I was all wet again. A different type of wetness from being soaked to the skin outdoors. Now, I was soaked within.

It was time for him to fuck me, and I wanted to say this, but I realised to my embarrassment that I didn't know his name. I felt a moment of panic, then decided it didn't matter. We had our agreement, our arrangement, and that bond of dealer to seller should have been all the information I needed. So I locked onto his clear green eyes and tilted my head toward the large bed in the centre of the room. He grinned, lifted me in his arms, and carried me to it.

There was romance in the gesture that pulled at me deep inside, from the base of my stomach to the split between my legs. Even though I was the same girl who had gotten off in the past by being taken in public, being tied down with leather thongs, bound with cuffs, spanked with paddles, fucked with dildos. Kink has always tended to make me come. But this time was different.

The thrill, I have always found, lies in the unknown. Plunging down those steps into darkness has always been my favourite way to play. Yet, usually, the need for danger takes me into extreme situations. This time, I found myself on a normal bed in an average hotel room, doing something extraordinary with a stranger.

"Trust me," he said, and I nodded.

The boy spread me out on the bed and continued with

his kissing games, making his way to the intersection of my body, then tracing a map of Amsterdam's canals around and around my clit. His tongue slid deep inside me, then pulled out, went back in to draw invisible designs on the inner walls of my cunt, and then out again, leaving me breathless and yearning.

"Now," I murmured, and he nodded, understanding. But then he moved off the bed again, rummaging through his pile of wet clothes until he found the bicycle lock and chain that he'd removed from my new cycle. Back at my side, he used the heavy metal links to bind my arms together over my head. No lock needed, just the chain wrapped firmly around my slender wrists. That was perfect, divine, just the type of rush that I craved.

Then, sitting up on the bed, he used his hands to part the slicked-up lips of my pussy, and his fingers slipped in my wetness. I sensed it a second before his cock pressed into me, and I stared into his eyes as we were connected. And oh, Christ, that feeling was almost overpowering, the length of his rod as he thrust deep inside me, following the same route made by his tongue moments before. Only now, I basked in the fullness of it. Thick and long, his cock filled me up.

Before I could even think about what I might want next, his fingers came back into play. He kept my pussy lips spread apart, stretching me open, and then the tips of his fingers began to tap out a sweet and unexpected melody over my clit. I sighed and ground my hips against him, letting him know how much I liked what he was doing. Then I squeezed him, from deep within, and this time he was the one to sigh. Open mouthed, eyes wide and staring into mine, he watched me for the whole ride. Held me with a gaze so intense that I couldn't look away.

This sent me over the edge. His fingers, his eyes, his

cock, his tongue all combining to take me there, to lift me up. To send me. My body closed in on his, and then opened up, squeezing and releasing, bringing him right up there with me. Pushing him over.

"Beauty," he whispered, stroking my still-wet hair away from my face as I came.

When I went downstairs later in the afternoon, the bike was gone, of course. "Your friend, he took it," the concierge told me with a smile. "But he left you this." The money was sealed in one of the cream-colored envelopes kindly provided by hotel. Fair trade. He knew I didn't really have use for a bike in Amsterdam, and if he'd taken the cash, that would have made him a whore instead of simply a street dealer. It was a wholly complete transaction, and I knew that I should have been satisfied.

Still, the next day found me walking through the city with a mission, pausing at each darkened alleyway until I heard the words that made me wet.

"Hey, pretty girl," he whispered, his voice low and seductive, "Wanna buy a bike?"

Damask Roses

When I have money, I will buy her flowers. She likes country roses, the kind that have rich, full blooms, petal-shades fading in various hues. She picks them, sometimes, from a garden in one of the upper-class neighbourhoods, late at night, when nobody is watching.

When I have money, I will take her to expensive hotels. I will rent the penthouse suite and order room service for her. Anything she wants. I will hire a masseuse to ease all the kinks from her muscles, to rub her body with almond oil until her skin has that golden shine of an ancient Egyptian goddess.

She doesn't ask me for anything, not anything like this. She simply smiles at me when she gets home from her job at the grocery store, sets her feet on our coffee table, and thanks me sweetly when I bring her a glass of cheap red wine.

We make love on the living room floor sometimes, with the curtains open so that moonlight fills the empty space. Her hair is a pale shade of red, almost pinkish like a tiger-striped kitty's. When the moonlight hits it, her hair seems woven with golden threads.

When I have money, she will wear gold. I will buy her strand upon strand and she will stand before the mirror, naked, save for those expensive knots of gold around her white throat. I will spread her on a bed filled with goose-down and make love to her while she wears those shining strands. They will sparkle in the tears that fill my eyes when I come. They will blend into her skin until it seems that she, herself, is woven of those magic threads.

She doesn't ask me for jewellery. She sits, with her feet on our wobbly coffee table, and she closes her eyes. I've worked all day, too, but I have more energy. I sink to my knees on the floor and I take her feet in my lap and I rub gently, lovingly, with my thumbs along the balls of her feet, in the dents of her arches, cupping her heels in my hands. She sighs, with her eyes still closed, and she says, "Oh, love, that feels good."

I run her a bath, next. I light candles on the ledge of the window and on the counter. When I have money, I will pour bottles of champagne to fill her tub. The bubbles will refresh her and they will make the secret, special place between her legs tingle and tickle. She'll squirm as the bubbles find their way inside her, and she'll laugh at me and touch my lips with her fingers.

When I dry her off, I will lick the champagne from the nape of her neck. I will lie her down on a snow-white bath towel and I will lap every drop of champagne from the valley of her stomach, from the lips of her sweetness, tonguing in between those lips to taste her own liquid, her own treasure.

She says she's fine with the cheap wine I can afford. She smiles at me when she sees the candles all around the tub, the candlelight hiding the crack in our mirror, the places in the wall where the tiles have fallen. She says she doesn't mind that we don't have money, that we can't travel to far away places, that we are still paying off school loans and car loans.

Sometimes, late at night, I sneak out of our bed and I

drive to the neighbourhood where the houses are big. Sometimes, I park my car and I walk along the sidewalks that line the park-size lawns. It's bad, I know, but I pick flowers from the gardens, flowers that I can never afford, and I hurry to my car and drive home so that she'll have roses by the bed when she wakes up. I want her to breathe in deeply in the morning and smell the rich, haunting fragrance of the roses that she adores.

At dawn, she stirs in my arms and she inhales and she smiles, still half-asleep, and she curls herself around me for warmth, finding my lips and kissing me until I am dizzy with want. I return her kisses. I part her lips with my own and play dancing games with her tongue. I kiss her cheeks and her eyelids and her earlobes. I make love to her face with my lips, leaving no part forgotten. She smiles as she falls back asleep. She presses her mouth to mine and she whispers, "Thank you."

And when I have money, she'll have roses all the time.

Your Hand

Zeke is a bartender at a restaurant that's so hip it doesn't even have a name, it only has an address on the outer concrete wall. In order to get a job at 68 Paradise Street, you have to be outrageously good-looking. Zeke fits the description. He's half German, half Native American and he has deep green eyes and straight black hair that hangs past his shoulder blades. When he's clean, he's like a living dream, so spectacular you're not sure you're actually looking at a real person and not an airbrushed fantasy.

When he's dirty, he's mine.

I'm a representative for one of the bigger vineyards in Sonoma. We make very good wine, which means that I don't have a difficult job at all. I bring my samples to the best restaurants and pour out tastes for the owners. They always order. My life is sweet.

Sometimes, owners ask the opinion of their favourite employees when they choose wine. If Zeke worked for you, you'd definitely ask his opinion. On wine. On food. On the way your hair smells. On the muscles that ripple across your stomach. On the position of your cock when it's hard. You'd get his opinion whenever you could. He's that kind of a guy. He makes you want to get close to him and hear him talk.

I met him on an afternoon at 68 Paradise when his young and rather podgy boss asked if Zeke would join us in a booth to taste my latest samples. Zeke sat across from me. His green eyes watched me. His full lips mesmerized me. His handsome face made it difficult for me to remember my name or the name of my wine or the reason I was sitting there, or where I had to go later in the evening.

Luckily, my job comes naturally for me. I served the samples, sold my wares, and gave Zeke my card. He surprised me by using it the same day, paging me, sending a shiver of anticipation through me that I hadn't felt in years.

It's not that I'm ugly or unused to the attention of attractive men. It's that I've never seen someone like Zeke before. I'm fine looking, myself. I'm tall, in shape, have dark hair that's greying at the temples. I dress in expensive suits when I'm selling and in faded jeans and crisp white T-shirts when I'm selling something else. I have no problem getting laid.

But I wanted this one. I wanted him, not for a one-night stand, but as a permanent fixture in my bedroom, over my kitchen table, on my balcony. And he called. He said he was intrigued. He apologised for staring at me in the restaurant, but said that I'd somehow managed to give him a raging hard-on while I spoke and he needed to see me.

This gave me an upper hand, somehow, and it allowed me to slow my beating heart and be the kind of man Zeke requires. A tough man. A strict man. A strong man. A dom man.

He came over after his shift, at almost three in the morning. I was ready, not in the least bit tired, and I saw then what I know now. Zeke is gorgeous when clean;

after working for eight hours at the furious pace of a bar like 68 Paradise, he is... he is... No words describe it except "changed". His skin is warmer and it has the scent of manly sweat on it. His muscles are alive beneath the golden canvas of his body. His eyes are darker green than in the light of day. He changes the way a vampire changes. Daylight holds him in its spell. At night, he comes alive.

"Could I shower?" he asked, "I came right over from the bar."

"No," I said, shaking my head to punctuate my statement. "No. I like you like this. You're mine like this. I want you just to strip and stand there."

My apartment is done entirely in white. There is a white rug, white walls, white sofa. I don't like the fussiness of colour. I like things stark. When Zeke stripped and stood still in the centre of my living room it was as if he were a piece of art on display in a museum. I couldn't contain myself. I walked around him, observing him, not touching him yet, but memorizing all parts of his body.

His cock was of mammoth proportions, beautifully crafted, hard as a piece of steel forced out and away from his body. He closed his eyes while I stared, but I told him to open them. He seemed at ease in his nakedness but confused by the way I was circling.

I said, "I've waited a long time for you. I want to learn how you look and work. I want to see you make yourself come so I can understand the changes in your face. I will educate myself on what you like and don't like. I will never forget what you need."

He didn't move.

I said, "You felt it at the bar and you know what I'm talking about. You and I are right for each other and I will control you and take you where you need to go. But like with any new purchase, the owner needs to read the manual. I want to know what you like and what it takes to make you come. You show me this one time, and I will never require a second lesson."

"You want me to jerk off?"

"Use your hand," I told him. "Use it the way you do when you're alone at home and it's been a long night and you need some release. Do it the way you've done since you were a teenager." I was talking through gritted teeth; I don't know why. The sound of my voice was unrecognisable to me, almost monotone, but I didn't care. I needed to see.

He slowly wrapped the fingers of his right hand around his throbbing cock. I took my breath in and held it while he began to stroke himself. I've never seen anything quite as beautiful as the spectacle of him standing naked and pleasing me with his own personal pleasure. Each stroke was a chord inside my head, a cymbal, an electric jolt.

He grew more comfortable with me as his audience and he closed his eyes and tightened his thigh muscles. I would have demanded he open his eyes at any other time, but if this was the way he did it at home, alone, solo, then I wouldn't fight him on it.

His strokes grew faster and rougher and I felt myself breathing hard and fast as if to match that speed. His hand became almost a blur, and the edge of his palm made a smacking sound against his skin each time he connected. It was something from an X-rated movie, something from my fantasy repertoire, something from a place older than time. He sucked in his breath between his teeth right before he erupted. His head went back and I wanted to go to him and hold him but I was frozen

149

where I stood, watching the come spurt from his cock, watching his hand slow, slow, stop.

"I'll learn," I said, as I came forward, as I bent on my knees to taste his liquid sex. "I'll learn every stroke and I'll memorize the way you play yourself."

He looked down at me, dark green eyes aware again, losing their afterglow quickly.

"I know," he said, sealing the bond between us. "I know."

Strangers

It burns when it goes down – the tequila, I mean – like fire. It burns me, but I smile at Katy, smile through the pain, and motion with my head for her to pour me another. And another. I'm not a masochist, but this is the kind of torture I like. Every sadist I know enjoys specific beats of pain, whether that means bowing occasionally to a Top even stronger than yourself, or taking the bits of it (like shards of broken crystal) when you can find it.

With Katy, though, it's not so much about pain but about power. That balance of it, even seen through eyes and vision gone unbalanced by the alcohol. We've got shot glasses lined up on the wooden dining room table, matching lines of frosted glass that indicate a race neither of us intends to lose.

In this game, there should be no losers.

Her hand touches mine when she pours the next round. Her fingertips slide against mine as the lip of the bottle chatters against the glass. "Glad I'm not driving," she says, a half-smile on her berry-stained lips.

"Wouldn't get far anyway," I tell her, motioning to the dark snow-filled streets outside. The ploughs haven't made it this far, so there's no one driving. No where to go.

"Yeah, but still." She picks up the glass and waits for

me to follow. I nod, lift mine, and we down them together. Four shots heating me darkly inside. I can see it working on her, as well, my little snow bunny, her cheeks flushed with pink, her sad, pale eyes glowing.

"I'm glad for the storm, too," she says softly, still smiling, but now looking a little coy – a bit of the flirt coming through. "I wouldn't have met you otherwise. I was planning on leaving before the last storm hit. But the added inches were too much to pass up."

Now I grin back at her. "You never know, do you? We could have been seated next to each other on the plane to New York. I might have slid my hand under the little airline blanket and played naughty games with you."

"You'd have done that? To a total stranger?"

"You're not a stranger."

That smile again, tinged with a pain I couldn't read. I wonder, for a second, if I can make that hurt go away. "I would have been. If we'd been seated next to each other on a plane."

"Oh." The tequila is already making me fuzzy. "I don't think you'd ever have been a stranger to me. I think I've always known you." And, with that graceless exchange, I gently kiss her wind-chapped lips.

Warmth, the sweet smell of the liquor, the crazy feel of her hair brushing my cheeks. There is always something magic about a first kiss, no matter how jaded and used a person might be. There will remain for ever something virginal and pure; dirty and secret; all swept together in a nameless, heart-racing emotion that makes you feel dizzy with want. Hungry with need.

Need. I need her. Need to take off her clothes, peel them off her body, reveal her. I've seen her only in two outfits: her black and neon-pink snow suit, and the faded denims and pale blue workshirt she changed into when we got here. But I need to see more, need to feel her skin growing flushed beneath the steady stroke, the silky caress, of my hands. In a rush, it comes. That desire. That yearning. Suddenly, and powerful, confusing to me.

I kiss her again. But that just makes it worse, and I end up pulling her into my lap, digging my hands into her hair, drinking those wet, violent kisses from her lips until she moans, bruised by the force of my desire. "Couldn't help it," I whisper. "Couldn't have stopped if I'd tried."

Call it the alcohol, the tequila that burns me. But you'll be lying if you do that, if you blame it on the liquor. I've craved her since the first glimpse I had as she stepped up in line for the ski lift, pushing her way ahead of a large group that hadn't wanted to be split up, and joining my solo tram to the top of the hill.

"Do you mind?" she'd asked, her breath in hazy puffs of silver grey, like smoke.

"No," shaking my head as the lift moved up, trying so hard to stifle the urge to kiss her right then. A captive audience. Nowhere for her to go but down. "No, 'course I don't mind."

Sometimes you can see it in the eyes of a stranger. You can see a need, a longing. And you know that you – only you – could fulfil the person's wants. But then they leave with their urges unspent, their longings unfulfilled, never knowing that you held the key. That you were the answer to their fantasies.

Her hand in the leather glove going forward to grasp mine. "Katy," she'd said, firmly shaking my hand up and down and waiting for me to offer my own name.

"Cleo."

I kept her hand in my paw, holding on for one beat too long, looking into her eyes which were blue at first, then grey. Which were sad and lonely. "My pleasure." Oh, yes, darling, my sole pleasure. *I could fix you*, I wanted to say. *I could make you whole again.*

"Lovely," she said, her voice suddenly softer. "The day, I mean." And I caught the rising colour at the base of her throat.

"Yes," I responded, mimicking her tone. "Yes, it is."

How I wanted to slide one finger into the ringed loop at the zippered neck of her jacket. How I wanted to pull down that zipper and reveal her, knowing somehow that seeing the shell of her skin would wreck me, devour me, consume me. I knew it all – I could visualize how pale her skin would look against the black of her snowsuit, how pink her nipples would be. Wanting to see the chill of the air bring a blushing hue to her all over. Bizarre. Dangerous to have those feelings for a total stranger.

But we weren't strangers for long.

Sliding down the hill, faster than usual for me – she's a better skier than I am – chugging up to the top again, then down to the bottom. Over and over, until, finally, breathlessly, I asked her if she'd have a drink with me.

Never know what someone will say to that. What they will take the request to mean. Does it mean only a drink? A polite smile and meaningless chat over tea or cocoa with those ridiculous tiny marshmallows bobbing around? Or does it mean: *I want to pour sweet red wine into the secret hollow parts of your body and then lick you clean.*

That's what I meant. That's what I wanted.

Fire. This woman set me on fire from the first look. Her radiant expression when she nodded and said "yes," then paused and, thinking out loud, said that she didn't like the bar in the clubhouse, would I mind going to her cabin.

Mind?

154

Fire. This woman, with her casual touch as she grabbed my hand and pulled me through the door and toward the four dark cabins that stood behind the club. Fire. This woman, who shivered as we walked and then gave me her generous smile as I played tough and offered her my coat. "Macho," she called me on it, poking fun at my act of chivalry and saying she'd rather warm up another way.

How?

"Tequila. Fire water. It's my favourite." A grin. A blush. "Not that I'm a lush," another grin, "But every once in awhile…"

And then the final storm hit. And I was saved.

"I came here to get myself together," she says now, breaking away from my kiss.

I don't respond. I only want more of her, more of her taste on my tongue, that fragrant mixture that is only a bit liquor and the rest her essence. I want to smell her everywhere, root like an animal between her legs to find her real core. I want to uncover the subtle difference between the scent of her hair and the secret place beneath her heavy tresses at the base of her neck. I want to spread her out on the bed and explore her, starting with her toes and working up – or beginning at her crown and working down. I don't care the order.

"I took a few days for myself to come here and ski. To get myself prepared for the battles, so to speak."

She's still in my lap, her head leaning on my shoulder, her cheek gently resting there. The weight of her in my arms makes me happy, and I take a deep breath and prepare myself to listen to her story, since she most obviously needs to share it. But then she surprises me.

"Another?" she asks, slipping two fingers under my chin and tilting my head down to hers. I think she means the alcohol, and I start to reach for the bottle when she says, "Another kiss, Cleo? Please?"

My mouth is open and on hers before the words are fully out of her mouth. I drink those sweet kisses from her parted lips, then pull back slightly to bite on her bottom lip.

"Ohhhhh," she sighs. Half-moan, half-breath, and I can feel her heart start to race. I lift her to a standing position and then up and into my arms, carrying her to the bed. Super-human strength filling me. Need filling me. Desire.

She regards me with her silvery eyes, the want in them an echo of my own lust. Not the liquor – you have to understand that – not the alcohol. Not two strangers alone in a room with no ties to each other, no weights on each other. Just want. Just need. Wrecking me, like I said. I knew it would. Watching as she undoes the buttons of her shirt and reveals her skin to me. Her soul to me. Baby, please, I want to beg her. Baby, please let me do it. You just lie there, let me do it, let me unwrap you like the precious gift you are. But I can't beg, because I'm in power in this game, and we both know it. (I don't know how we know it. It just is.)

She parts her shirt, then slides out of the sleeves. Now she only has jeans on, worn so roughly that they fit her body like a thin veneer. In a second, she has the fly unbuttoned, the faded blues down and off and kicked into a heap on the floor. I'm dressed, and she is all pretty and naked, wearing only a lazy grin and an open embrace.

I can't even wait to get my own clothes off. I go for her still dressed, still wearing my black silk turtleneck and black leggings. Pretty thing, that's all I can think to call her. Innocent on that bed, in the pink light shining through the scarf she's draped over the light. I can't wait

– I keep saying it, but I want to explain the rush – like powering down the hill at full speed – the need to taste her, to plunge my tongue inside her, where she is all warm and wet and secret – to drink that fragrant honey in, to taste her on the tip of my tongue…

Another half-moan, half-scream, this time. Her fingers twining in my dark hair, her body arching into an S-curve, pressing her hips up to my lips, my hands going underneath her, gripping into her waist, lifting up so I can eat her like fruit, so I can devour her.

She helps me, she becomes even lighter somehow in my embrace. But then it's like holding onto a cloud, or a spirit, how quickly she slips through my fingers and turns herself on the bed, going for me, sliding her hands under the waistband of my silk long johns and pulling them down. No, I want to. I want to take care of her. All I want in the world is to erase the hurt that lingers in her pale eyes. Someone else's hurt. Someone else left that look there.

I said before, I'm the sadist, the Top, the one in power. But it doesn't always work like that, with one in charge and the other following, accepting. It doesn't always have to be like that. Sometimes it's more of a dance, a dance with two well-trained partners equally in charge. Equally responsible. That's how it is with her, the way she turns herself and moves to take me into her embrace. The way she slides with the same grace she exposed on the slopes, slides in my arms and positions herself in a side-sixty-nine, bodies pressed against each other, but neither one of us on top.

Her tongue mimics mine, playing all those twisting, twirling games. Being gentle, at first, then working up to it. To the pounding motions, the deeper thrusts. I bring my fingers into the action, and she does as well. I part her lips, revealing her, using my thumb and forefinger to expose her clit. She moans, the sound so lovely, captured against me, and suddenly her actions slow, slow, cease, her mouth still pressed to my cunt, but her tongue frozen. She is mesmerized by what I am doing to her. I have found her secrets, figured out the code. And it gives me an inordinate amount of pleasure to take her higher, to take her where she so needs to go.

I move away for only a second, having her roll onto her back and taking my spot between her legs. As I do, I see the look in her eyes, that haunted look, has changed to one of longing. Her lips open and then close, wordlessly, begging me to continue.

Oh, yes, my darling. My angel. My snow bunny. I will. I will make everything better.

So fast, it happened, the wind rushing me as we rode in the lift – so fast, her beating heart setting the pace. And I only wanted to take her, to take her higher. To take her where she most needed to go.

You can see it sometimes, in the eyes of a stranger. You can see that need, that longing. And know that you – only you – could fulfil the person's wants. But then they leave, walk out of the elevator. Off the bus. Away from the curb. They leave with their urges unspent, their longings unfulfilled, never knowing that you held the key. That you were the answer to their fantasies.

But I am to her.

And I turn that key.

And I open her door.

The Sex Test

My best friend Roxanne and I share everything, from secrets to lipstick to the occasional man. Years ago, we had keys made to each other's apartments, for those times when I'm out of town and she really needs to borrow one of my leather jackets. Or the occasions when I want to lift one of her treasured Led Zeppelin LPs and she doesn't answer her page. We lend, give, and trade items all the time. So when she brought over a stack of fashion magazines that she'd finished reading, I thought nothing of it.

Still, there *was* something odd about the way she handed over the magazines to me. A subtle rosy blush coloured her normally pale, freckled skin. A strangely charged heat shone in her dark green eyes, and she ducked her head rather than staring at me straight on when she offered them over. There was a nervous, jittery quality to her behaviour that I'd never seen before. I ignored the signs that something bizarre was going on because I simply didn't understand. At least, not until much later that night.

"Don't worry about giving them back, Lisa," she told me. "I'm finished."

I hefted the weighty stack of magazines, then fanned out the top few, looking them over. She had all the girly genres covered – a gossip sheet, a magazine devoted to cosmetics, a fancy foreign number featuring a partially nude model on the cover, and a famous magazine devoted to helping women transform themselves for men. I would never buy any of these for myself, and Roxy knew it.

"They're just fluff," she continued, sounding somewhat embarrassed. Then as if she couldn't help herself, she added, "But maybe you'll learn something." She motioned with a casual nod of her head to my faded Levis and standard long-sleeved white T-shirt. I'm no risk-taker when it comes to my wardrobe. I like the clean lines of jeans and a tank top, the soft caress of well-worn leather, or sharp-looking suits when I need to dress up.

Roxy's the opposite. We are both long and lean, but Roxanne tends to dress more exotically, choosing splashier colours, tighter fits. She's gone through all the phases – punk, femme, even the military look that was the rage again this year. On her, I have to say that all the different styles have worked. Her attitude takes her through, and sometimes I'm even tempted to join her on a fashion adventure. Nobody but Roxy could get me to wear high heels instead of my normal Doc Martins, but she's done it. No one but my best friend could cajole me into wearing a bright lipstick red sarong at the beach, and Roxy's done that, too.

"Have fun," she grinned, watching as I stacked the magazines on my modern glass coffee table. "I'll call you tomorrow."

After she left, I got comfortable on the white leather sofa in my living room, perusing the various magazines in the fading summer sunlight. Outside my open window, I could hear the sounds of happy voices overlapping, couples giggling together on the gold-flecked sands of

160

the Santa Monica Beach. On my own that Friday evening, I was thrilled to have such mindless reading matter to fill my time. It would keep thoughts away from the fact that I was dateless.

The first magazine was a slim volume filled with pages of flirty outfits and a whole slew of tips for keeping a man. I flipped through that magazine in no time. I know how to keep men, and as I said before, flirtatious clothes aren't really my thing. The second, a European fashion edition, took me longer. I daydreamed my way through the 400 plus pages, pictured myself in the different designer suits, tried to imagine which pieces would look better on me and which would be more flattering to Roxanne. Not difficult at all. She'd wear the beaded ball gowns, the fantastic, frilly confections made of fluttering lace. I'd accompany her in the sleek black suits, the wide-legged crepe chine pants, the butter-soft black leather.

By the time I'd visualized each of us in all of the different outfits, it was getting late, and I decided to move to my bedroom. First, I poured myself a glass of chilled white wine, then stripped down to a white tank top and a pair of gray silk boxers. In my room, I slid beneath the covers of my bed and reached for magazine number three. This was a famous one, known for articles filled with sexual ideas, innuendos, and reader confessions. I consider it the equivalent of eating some brightly-coloured drugstore candy. Not necessarily good for you, but oh so sweet. It was also something I'd never read if Roxy didn't give it to me.

I worked my way through slowly, as if reading about an alien culture. As I flipped the glossy pages, I learned about the proper way to wear sheer pink lipgloss (as if I'd ever wear pink), read the amazing statement that "navy blue is the new black" – I still don't get that – before finally coming to a quiz in the very centre of the magazine. "How Much of a Risk Taker Are You Beneath the Sheets?" The headline queried. Below, was the subheading: "What Your Secret Fantasies Reveal About You."

Well, I'm not a risk taker at all. I didn't need a stupid quiz to tell me that. I'm the type to weigh my options, dipping my toes in the shallow end to test the temperature first. It takes a while for me to make decisions, and once I do, my mind is set. But before I could simply turn the page and move on, I noticed that Roxanne had already filled out the questionnaire. She'd used a fine red pen, circling the different letters of the multiple choice answers. Even though we're very different, I thought that I'd test myself by reading her answers. I wondered whether I would be able to guess the way she would respond to each query. That was the *real* test.

I hesitated for a moment before starting. Would she want me to know her innermost fantasies? Were there any that I didn't know already? No, I thought not. Roxanne and I tell each other everything, don't we? This would simply be a fun way for me to exercise my brain power, trying to guess how she would fill in a silly sex test.

The first question jumped right into the subject matter: *Choose the fantasy that most describes your hidden desire. A) Taking the upper hand in a bedroom situation. B) Sharing the power with a partner. C) Letting your lover set the stage.*

C was circled twice.

Hmmm. That one took me by surprise. My instincts told me that she'd have chosen A, for sure. Roxanne has the type of firecracker personality that often accompanies bright red hair and golden-freckled skin. I'd assumed that she would be the one on top in any situation – between the sheets or otherwise. With a bit more interest, I read on. Yes, I continued to feel a little guilty for snooping, but not guilty enough to stop.

Question two asked the test-taker to put the following fantasies in order, with the one that was the most arousing at the top.

Role playing
Exhibitionism
Voyeurism
Food play
Bondage

Roxanne hadn't bothered ranking them at all, as if the concept didn't interest her in the slightest. Instead, underneath the different choices, she'd written in the indecipherable statement: *being found out.*

Now what did that mean – and why would it be a turn-on?

I took another sip of wine, considered calling her and asking her about her answers, and then decided to simply keep on reading. This was the most exciting stuff I'd found all night.

The next part of the quiz was made of several phrases, requiring the reader to mark as T for True or F for False. *I have participated in the following activities:*

Played with sex toys
Acted out role-playing fantasies
Tried a ménage à trois
Experienced with bondage
Been with another woman

Each statement had a "T" next to it, again surprising me greatly and the final one had an exclamation point written in by hand. From sharing stories in the past, I knew that Roxanne was in no way a tentative lover. She'd told me about the time she took her panties off in the window of a cafe on Main Street. Without thoughts of reprisals, she'd spread her slim legs so that her date would be able to see her naked, pantyless pussy when he returned from feeding the meter. He'd paid the check immediately, hurrying her out behind the restaurant for a bit of public sex in the parking lot. So excited that he couldn't even wait until they got home. Which was exactly what Roxanne had been hoping for.

Then there was the lover who liked to dress her up. They'd often enjoyed decadent fantasies come to life in the guise of a headmistress and naughty pupil, or kinky nurse and shy patient. She had thrown herself into the fun of make believe, dragging me along with her to thrift stores on Melrose in search of the perfect costumes.

"I need a cheerleader skirt," she'd confessed. "Something short and pleated."

We'd spent hours perusing the racks at all of our favourite haunts until she'd come up with the perfect red and white number. "Dan's going to flip when he sees this," she'd said, pleased, before correcting herself. "Well, I'm going to flip, and he's going to come."

Roxanne never seemed to feel awkward talking about sex with me. She'd even called me late, late one night, needing to immediately share an encounter she'd had with two of her co-workers. After a late, stressful meeting at the ad agency, the threesome had gone out drinking to one of Roxanne's favourite high-end bars. From the top floor of a hotel, they had watched Malibu burning. It was that season when brushfires plagued this most wealthy of communities. Something about watching the destruction of all that valuable real estate had given

Roxy the nerve to come on to both of the handsome co-workers. They'd gotten a room in the hotel downstairs, and these lucky men had spent several hours making her sexual sandwich fantasy come true, with Roxy in between as the filling.

But somehow even knowing all of these stories from her past, I'd never have guessed that she'd been with a girl. Or that she'd tried any sort of bondage. I couldn't envision her captured, her wild, untamed spirit reined in. Where had I been? Had she tried to tell me but felt that I wasn't receptive?

I was anxious to find out what else I'd missed hearing about. Yet for another moment, a stab of guilt at reading the quiz stopped me. How would I feel if Roxy had stumbled on my own filled-in questionnaire? That was an easy question to answer: I'd never take an idiotic test like this, wouldn't think to waste my time on one. If I had, though, I wouldn't mind Roxy reading my answers. There was nothing about me that she didn't know already. So taking another sip of wine, I quickly got over my moral issues and plunged on.

Question four was about dirty movies. Next to the titles were brief write-ups, in case the questioned hadn't seen the flick. I'd seen them all. Apparently, Roxanne had, as well.

Which erotic movie would you most easily see yourself starring in:

Basic Instinct (Dominant woman)
9 1/2 Weeks (Submissive woman)
Bound (Lesbian relationship)

The second and the third titles were underlined, letting me know that she wanted to try a submissive role in a girl-girl relationship. And suddenly instead of simply acting like a private detective, peeking into my friend's hidden fantasy life, I found myself getting aroused.

Oh, Roxanne, I thought. *You naughty, naughty girl.*

Suddenly, the way she'd acted earlier in the evening made sense to me. She'd been revealing herself in an unexpected manner. Carefully, cautiously. And that wasn't like my Roxanne at all. A born risk taker, she was used to spelling things out clearly from the start. With any other potential lover, she'd have been bold and outspoken. Not with me. The lengths she'd gone through to get into my mind were both surprising and flattering. How she'd book-ended the magazine between the others, using them as merely innocent props, knowing that I'd reach for this one later in the night, guessing easily my routine of climbing into bed to enjoy the fluffy volume.

Oh, Roxanne, I thought again. *You aced that quiz, didn't you? You're the number one risk taker of all. Go to the front of the class, girl.*

But what did it all mean? She was coming on to me. That was for sure. Yet why hadn't we gone this route before? She knows full well that I like both men and women, and she also knows that I play the top role whenever I can. My personality may not be that of a standard risk-taker, for I am methodical in my dealings. From my work to my social life, I enjoy order, calm, and the power of being in charge. It floods through me in a rush, from my very centre outward to the edges of my body. Bringing someone else to that highest point of pleasure, being in charge of their fulfilment, that's what makes me cream. And if submitting is a turn-on for a lover, it works well with my need for dominance.

Sprawling back against the pillows, I slid a hand under my nightshirt, finding the waistband of my charcoal silk boxers and then stroking myself lazily through the material. My thoughts were entirely of Roxanne, of me and Roxanne, playing the way she obviously wanted to play.

In my fantasy, I saw Roxanne letting go. Tied, or cuffed, to my bed, her supple body trembling, her head turning back and forth on my pillow, that long, glossy hair of hers spread in a fiery mane against my white sheets. And I saw myself, not undressed yet, still wearing a pair of my favourite faded jeans, a tight white tank top that perfectly fit my lean, hard-boned physique, and holding something in my hand. Closed my eyes tighter, as if that would make the image come clearer to me. Ah, yes, it was a crop, and I was tracing the tip of the beautiful weapon along her ribs, down the basin of her concave belly. A belly I've admired so many times in dressing rooms, or out at the beach, although never have I let my fantasies get away from me.

Now, I did, seeing it my mind as I parted her pretty pussy lips and sliding the braided edge of the crop up inside her, getting it nice and wet.

My hand pushed my boxers aside, needing direct finger-to-clit contact. Slowly, but firmly, I made dreamy circles around and around. And I thought about Roxanne's tongue there, working me when I finally joined her on the bed. She'd still be tied. Bound to my silver metal bed frame. But her tongue would be free to act how it wanted to. I'd bring my hips in front of her, use my own fingers to part my nether lips, let her get a good look at me inside before allowing her to kiss my cunt.

When she was ready, and I was dripping, I would press myself against her face, would let her tongue-fuck me until I could hardly take the pleasure. Only then would I turn around, slide into a sixty-nine, rewarding her with the beauty of a well-earned orgasm. I'd eat her until her whole body trembled, slip my tongue up inside her, paint invisible pictures on the inner walls of her pussy –

Suddenly I stopped. Stopped touching myself. Stopped fantasizing. What if I was wrong? What if she had simply filled out the quiz for the hell of it, had forgotten all about it and given the magazine to me in perfect innocence. What if I was the one reading things into this, making the wrong assumptions? Yes, it looked as if we'd be prime mates in the bedroom, but maybe that wasn't what Roxanne had in mind at all. Hell, maybe she hadn't even been the one to take the quiz.

Feeling an unexpected sense of panic burst through me, I reached for the magazine again, skimming the remaining questions for signs that Roxanne was the test-taker, and that she'd been answering the queries for my eyes only. It didn't take me long to find the proof I needed. There, as usual, at the end of the quiz, were the directions for tallying the results, followed by three different write-ups explaining the scores: Cool-headed vixen, Hot-blooded mama, and Bungee-jumping bad-ass babe.

A heavily-handed X had been drawn fiercely through the three different write-ups, and Roxanne had inserted a new one in her careful handwriting in the margin. It said, "Frisky Femme Feline: Loves her friends, and loves to take risks, but sometimes doesn't have the guts to say what she wants. Which is this: You. I want you, Lisa. Call me and let me know if you will play the way I like. Will you?

Would I?

Now, it was my turn to forget my careful, plodding manner, my style of weighing all facts and figures before making a decision. Roxanne's cell number is programmed into my phone's memory, and I reached for the handset and pressed the one key on my speed dial. Maybe she wouldn't be there – she'd said she had plans for the night – but I'd leave a message.

Turns out, I didn't have to. She answered on the very first ring, as if she'd been waiting for my call.

"It's me," I told her.

"Hey, Lisa," she said, her voice ultra-casual. She didn't know if I'd read the test. That was obvious from her tone.

"Where are you?"

"Why?"

"How soon can you be here?"

Now, I heard her laughing, relief in the quickness and ferocity of her giggles, and then I heard another noise that made my heart race. The front bell. She was right outside. A risk-taker to the very end. Risking her heart. Putting herself out for potential embarrassment, but probable pleasure.

Tossing the phone on the bed, I hurried to the front door, just as she let herself in with her spare key. Through the open doorway, I saw from the scattering of cigarette butts that she'd been sitting outside on my front porch the whole time, waiting, hoping. The thought that she'd pictured me reading her fantasies turned me on even more than I already was. What would she have done if she'd known I was touching myself while fantasizing about her?

"Get inside," I said, motioning with my head toward the bedroom. But we didn't make it that far. We couldn't. Roxanne and I only had the patience to shut the door, to stop in the centre of my living room and reach for each other. My hands working quickly to undress her. Hers helping me as we got her T-shirt off, pulled down her faded cut-offs, revealed the wonder of her body as she kicked out of the navy lace thong she had beneath.

"Navy's the new black," I muttered to her as I pulled my own clothes off.

She gave me a quizzical look, but didn't speak.

"That's one of the things I learned from your magazines."

As I spoke, I pushed her back against the leather sofa, making her knees bend as she sat and then going on the floor in front of her. Unlike the cool quality of my fantasy, the steely way in which I held out her pleasure until the end, I needed my mouth on her pussy immediately, needed her taste on my tongue, her sweet, tangy juices spread over my skin. Slow and steady, as always, I worked her. She was divine, sublime, her creamy nectar like nothing I'd ever tasted before. The way she moved, her hips sliding forward, her hands in my short hair. Every touch, every moan let me know how right we were together.

Now, that we were really in synch, I found that I could start to relax. Roxy was almost desperate, yearning, wanting me to let her climax. I decided I would, if she could answer my questions. Lifting my lips away from her sex, I started off.

"You want my mouth against your pussy –"

"Oh, yes."

"Let me finish," I admonished her, and when I looked up into her eyes, I saw that she was paying me careful attention. "A) you want my mouth against your pussy, or B) you want to roll over on your stomach and let me play back there."

Roxy sighed hard, understanding what I was offering, and she answered by moving her body, rolling onto her stomach and pressing her face against the smooth surface

170

of my leather sofa. Quickly, I parted her rear cheeks, touching her hole with my tongue. Just a touch, but I felt the electrifying shudder that slammed through her body. Roxy, my bad girl, loves to be explored like that. My fingers up in her snatch, my tongue probing and teasing. I ate her from behind for several minutes, and when I was ready to move on, I leaned back and asked question number two.

"You planted the test where I could find it –"

Again she interrupted me, sighing the word, "Yes," as if it were an entire sentence. "Yessssss."

"Not finished, baby," I told her, and she shook her head, as if she knew she'd done something wrong. I could tell that she was dazed by the proximity of her orgasm, and that was exactly why I wanted to keep teasing her. My main talent in bed is the ability to hold off. To force myself to wait for that final release, and to help my lovers wait for it, as well. Anticipation is my favourite aphrodisiac.

"You planted the test where I could find it –" I said again, watching as Roxy bit her bottom lip to keep herself from responding too early. "Rather than simply telling me what you wanted because you thought that I might punish you for playing dirty."

"Oh, true," Roxanne purred. "True, Lisa. True."

That was all I needed to hear. I brought one hand against her ripe, lovely bottom, spanking her hard on her right cheek, then giving her a matching blow on the left. Roxanne sucked in her breath, but didn't move, didn't squirm or try to get away. How pretty my handprints looked against her pale skin. I wanted to further decorate her, but I couldn't keep myself from parting her cheeks again and kissing her between. Roxanne could hardly contain herself now. The spark of pain mixed with the pleasure confused and excited her, and she ground her hips against the edge of my sofa, wordlessly begging for something.

For more.

I gave her more. Alternating stinging, sharp spanks with sweet, French kisses to both her ass and her pussy, sliding my mouth down along her most tender, private regions, pushing her further toward the limits of her pleasure.

Then, once again, I stopped all contact, sensing exactly the right moment to ask the final question on my own, personal Sex Test.

"Oh, yes, Lisa," Roxanne whispered as the pleasure rose within her.

"You're about to come on my tongue," I said a sliver away from her skin just before I brought her closer to climax. "True or false?"

Lost In The Translation

"What did she say?" I whispered to Johnny, staring at the angry flush of heat in Birgit's cheeks.

Johnny shook his head. Together we were lost in a foreign world. Whenever our friends wanted to talk privately, they simply reverted to their native tongue of German, instantly plunging the two of us into helplessness. How could we get involved in a conversation that we didn't understand? So we watched them bleakly, and waited in silence, knowing that eventually they would translate.

This evening, Birgit was the one who finally explained the situation. She wanted to take us out to her favourite restaurant. Wolf wanted to show us the red light district. The decision was up to us, and there was no way of guessing what had been lost in the translation. As could be expected, Johnny instantly voted for Wolf's plan, squeezing my hand hopefully. I agreed, curious myself, and the four of us drove to the Reeperbahn.

Once there, we wandered along the sidewalks, glancing in shop windows and observing the erotic sights until the harsh throb of a foreign phrase caught my attention. Unlike the flurry of normal conversations floating around us, these words were different, a come-on directed at me.

"What did he say?" I asked Birgit, who had been designated as my perverted tour guide for the evening.

"The women in there," she began, indicating the darkened doorway that led to a hidden strip club, "they're all of legal age. But they're shaved, so they look younger." Then she pulled me along at a trot because we'd fallen behind the boys.

I glanced back at the heavyset barker, who winked at me before continuing his fast-talking German spiel, hawking his human wares to any passers-by, even well-dressed girls like us. *What use would we have for shaved strippers?* I wondered, but the sinful gleam in his eyes made me feel instantly dirty, as if he knew all of my secrets. As if he might call them out to the next customer.

Swiftly, we fell into place behind our boyfriends, who were oblivious to the fact that we'd dropped back from them. Both men were fully captivated by the line of attractive prostitutes standing nonchalantly across the street from the police station. Our little foursome was clearly connected, but this didn't stop the hustling women from approaching anyone with a cock. Each girl had a different move – a sensual head nod, seductive lower lip lick, an air kiss. Some were far bolder than that, stepping forward to actually speak to Johnny and Wolf, making pointed conversation in their lilted, foreign tongue.

"What did *she* say?" I hissed to Birgit after a kitten-like blonde in sleek leopard-print slacks and a zipper-encrusted leather top spoke to my beau.

"She asked if he was interested," Birgit told me, translating the words without hesitation. "She said that she's the best – too good to pass up. Better than his wife." This last bit made Birgit's eyes narrow, as if she couldn't believe the nerve. I watched Johnny carefully for his response. While Wolf rephrased the proposition in English, Johnny looked the prostitute up and down, as if he were actually considering the offer. In my mind, I tried to imagine what Johnny could possibly whisper to me so that I'd let him go and experience "the best".

"We're only here for a few days," he'd say. "And we *did* agree that we wanted to savour all of the international delights before returning home."

Then I'd give him a kiss and tell him, "Sure, baby. Enjoy yourself. Here's a handful of Deutschmarks. Have a blow job on me."

As if reading my thoughts, Johnny turned around and gave me a sheepish smile, letting me know that he was simply a tourist on a sex-charged ride. *No problems, honey*, his expression said. *No worries*. On we went, heading toward the main drag of the Reeperbahn, where Birgit told us we could watch dirty movies, visit the erotic art museum, hear a late-night concert, buy a gun, fulfil any one of our decadent appetites. But before we reached the corner, Wolf stopped.

"No, Wilfried," Birgit said immediately. She was calling him by his full name, which showed me how serious she was. "Don't do it."

"He'll never get another chance," Wolf told her.

Birgit shook her head fiercely. Once again, our German hosts engaged in a short, heated discussion in their own language. Johnny and I stood with raised eyebrows and listened to the friends we'd known since grad school. What wouldn't Johnny get a chance to do? And why wouldn't Birgit want him to have that opportunity? Birgit shrugged angrily, as if to say "do what you want", and Wolf said in his perfect, unaccented English, "Leave it up to them, right?" and Birgit nodded, blue eyes blazing.

"There's a street," Wolf began. "Where the women are."

I knew that he was leaving out something important, because as far as I could tell, the "women" were everywhere. Turning my head, I spotted several prostitutes moving in our direction. One statuesque brunette was wearing gold hot-pants and lace-up boots, not even shivering while the rest of us were bundled against the chill. Apparently, she had an internal heater. Johnny and I waited silently for further explanation.

"Down there," Wolf said, indicating a glossy, scarlet-painted gate that towered over our heads. "Behind those doors, there is a street where only men can go."

"Why?" I asked, my shoulders tightening automatically.

"They don't want the competition," Birgit explained. "Or simply curiosity-seekers. They want customers. Males mean sales."

"Would you like to go?" Wolf asked. His tone made it apparent that *he* was the one who really wanted to take that stroll. "Just to look," he continued. "They sit in the windows and you choose."

"It's nothing," Birgit said, shaking her head. "Sluts under glass. That's all." But Johnny wanted a peek, I could tell, and so could Wolf. "I hate that we can't go, too," Birgit muttered, revealing genuine frustration. "If they're so good, they should be able to handle another woman walking by."

But they wouldn't want to compete with a girl like Birgit – that was my instant thought. So lovely, with her long, blonde hair fanning loose over her black cashmere sweater. Bright blue scarf tight around her throat. Pale blue gloves matching her suede slacks. She was far prettier than any of the stunners we'd seen so far, and she gave Wolf what he wanted for free. Although, from the furious expression on her face, I thought he might not be getting any tonight.

Johnny looked at me, a question beating in his deep green eyes, and I nodded. Who was I to keep him from a once-in-a-lifetime journey?

"How long will it take?" I asked.

"An hour," Wolf promised. "Maybe less."

He wouldn't meet my gaze as he spoke. Was there something else in the plan, something that Wolf wasn't telling me?

"We'll see you back at home," Birgit said suddenly, surprising me by how easily she was giving up. "I'm going to take our little one here out drinking. She's never had a Hefeweizen, if you can believe it. Don't worry. We'll cab." Wolf grinned like a kid, obviously thrilled that his girlfriend had acquiesced. Had he never been allowed down the street before? I didn't have time to ponder that, because the boys were moving in speeded-up motion before we could change our minds. I watched Wolf open the red gate, saw the two men disappear behind the wall. Then Birgit was tugging my hand, pulling me toward a waiting taxi.

"Where's the bar?" I asked as we settled ourselves in the plush leather interior.

"We're not going to a bar. We're going down that street," Birgit said forcefully, her ice blue eyes gleaming. "It'll just take a little doing."

Back at their Hamburg apartment, Birgit riffled through Wolf's wardrobe. "We need guy clothes," she said, "and hats. We're lucky it's winter. Less exposed skin means less exposed features." I stood, bottle of beer in hand, as I watched her gather what she wanted. Honestly, I wasn't that interested in seeing women behind windows, but I was excited at the prospect of an adventure. Besides, I liked the way Birgit moved, telling me what to do and how to act. It meant that I didn't have to make any decisions.

"You'll need to tape those," she told me, indicating my full chest with a casual motion as she tossed over a roll of bandages. I'm slim, but I have curves. "Get yourself as flat as you can."

Now that it was really happening, my heart started to race. *Go fast*, I thought. *Don't think*. Modestly, I faced away from her as I pulled off my shirt and sweater and started to roll the bandage around my breasts. But Birgit moved next to me, helping, her fingers cold on my warm skin as she tucked in the end of the bandage.

"Wipe off your make-up," she told me. "No lipstick. No liner." I retreated to the bathroom to follow her orders, then returned, clean-scrubbed and fresh-smelling, although feeling something like a mummy in the bandage.

"Perfect," she said. "Now a button-up shirt, I think. Good that you're so tall. Makes things easier." She cocked her head, looking me over. "Keep on the jeans, but put on a pair of my docs. Your boots are too femme." I followed her commands, fingers trembling as I did the laces up on her heavy black shoes. "Leather jacket," she said to herself, nodding. "And some hat. Baseball hat? Yes, Johnny's got one, right?" As if on automatic pilot I found myself in the guest room, grabbing Johnny's vintage ball cap from the dresser and putting it on backwards.

"Your short hair is a godsend," Birgit said, fussing impatiently with her own intense silky, blonde mane. She wrapped it tightly, tucked the length down her turtleneck collar, and then grabbed a striped woollen hat. She'd dressed similarly to me, but without needing to wrap her small breasts. Standing side-by-side in front of the mirror, we looked like two young boys.

"If anything," she said, "they'll hassle us for being underage. We need something else." She rummaged a bit more, and then ran into the kitchen, coming back with a pack of Wolf's Marlboro Reds. Our friends smoke American brands, while we think we're cool to buy the European ones.

"Smoking will keep our hands busy and give us something to cover our faces."

Again, we stood in front of the mirror, staring. Then Birgit snapped her fingers and said, "I know. I know –" and she reached into Wolf's dresser and pulled out two socks. "Roll 'em up and stick 'em down," she instructed, and soon there we stood: two insecure youths with smoking habits and serious hard-ons. "Let's go."

The cab ride was a tense five minutes as I tried to decide whether or not I could go through with this bizarre charade. "What happens," I whispered, "if they realise we're girls?"

"They'll throw ice water on us," she said matter-of-factly, "and bits of garbage."

That sounded like a whole lot of no fun.

"Maybe we should just go to the bar," I suggested softly, struggling to find a comfortable way to breathe with my chest so firmly wrapped. "We could have another heffer-whatever –"

"No," Birgit had her mind set. "This is it," she told the cab driver, and he murmured something back to her as he handed over the change. Birgit responded with a dark, smoky chuckle that sounded nothing like her normal laugh.

"What did he say?" This was my mantra for the evening.

"He said, 'Have a good night, gentleman,'" Birgit grinned, pushing me out the door. Then there we were, back in front of the red gates.

"What if Johnny and Wolf find out?" I asked, my last ditch effort to talk sense into my friend.

"What can they possibly say?" she responded. "They've already done it. And who knows what else —"

She was right, and I took a deep breath and followed her through the gate and into another world. Instantly, I saw that we were in a sort of human sex mall. Lining both sides of the narrow street were tiny storefronts with floor-to-ceiling windows. Behind most windows sat a woman, waiting. I was surprised to see that the windows were actually lit with stark red light bulbs — hence the term 'red light district'. Each window held a comfortable-looking chair, like an old-fashioned recliner. The chairs were decorated in a variety of different styles. Some had flags draped lushly over the seats. Others featured more luxurious fabrics, comforters made of velvet and satin.

As we strolled by, I noticed that several windows were dark. These were the ones that had customers, Birgit explained. "It's early," she said, looking around at the light pedestrian traffic. "Men with their needs come out later in the evening." But although this meant that there were many women for us to look at, this also meant that we were scrutinized as potential customers by each one. Some waved. Some stood in open doorways and beckoned. I could see their eyes, the red embers of their cigarettes, their bodies encased in shiny, revealing clothing.

"Hey, tall dark and handsome, come back —" one

called, and I wondered how she knew I spoke English, and then remembered my baseball cap with the SF Giants logo on it. A clever guess. As we wandered, I looked out for Wolf and Johnny, but there was no sight of our mates.

"The boys are long gone," Birgit said. "They scurried down fast."

Turning to look at her, I understood in a mental flash that she was smarter than Wolf, that when he played his little boy games with her, she was always the one in charge. "All macho in front of us," she continued, "but when women are offering sex for real, they get scared."

Maybe, I thought, *but maybe not.* I peered into the hazy grey of one storefront as we strolled by. *Maybe they're each behind one of those darkened windows.*

Because there are things that you can't translate. Expressions. Wounds from old secrets. And there are some things that don't require translation – like the fact that I knew Johnny would sleep with one of the prostitutes if he had the chance, that I knew he'd done so before. Nuances like the heat between me and Birgit, the questioning glances, sly smiles, accidental brushes up against one another. You don't need a phrase book to understand certain concepts even if they are foreign as of yet. Even if you've never done them before.

At the end of the block, we turned around, walking faster down the other side until we reached the starting place. Now that we'd actually succeeded, there was no need to linger. Birgit smiled at me, and herded me through the gate.

"We did it," she said, gripping onto my hand tightly.

My cigarette had burned down to the filter, becoming one long piece of silvery ash. Birgit plucked the butt from my fingers and crushed it out on the concrete sidewalk. Then she took a step closer to me. Her breath was icy. Puffs of wispy frozen air. Behind her, the barker called out to us.

"What did he say?" I asked, desperately.

"He said that his girls inside are young and pretty and shaved." She paused before adding her own opinion in a different tone of voice, "But they're not as pretty as you." As she said the words, she kissed me. Her cold lips pressed to mine, and I felt her arms pull me forward. Wrapped in her tight embrace, her sock cock jammed into my side.

"Is that a tube sock in your pocket?" I whispered, "or are you happy to see me?"

She laughed hard, her real laugh, and then took my hand again, pulling me back to the taxi stand where a line of cabs waited. "They won't be back yet," she predicted. "If Wilfried thinks I took you drinking, then he knows he has a couple of hours to kick around town with Johnny. They're probably in one of the kino houses."

"Kino?"

"Movie. *Dirty* movies on this street. Two men, jacking off in the darkness."

I didn't have to ask what we were going to do. Her fingers played with mine on the ride home, squeezing. The cab driver kept his eyes intently on the rear-view mirror, watching.

"He thinks we're fags," Birgit said, pulling her woollen cap off to reveal her long honey-blonde mane. The driver seemed to visibly relax. And then Birgit wrapped one arm around my neck and pulled me in for our second kiss. Sweet, at first, and then hot as her lips parted and her tongue met mine.

"Here –" she said, just when I was losing myself in the wonder of it all. "Right here." She paid the driver and hurried me back up the four flights of steps to the apartment. There were no words then. Just Birgit unwrapping me as if I were a Christmas present. My hat off. Sweater on the floor. Long strand of bandages unwound and discarded. Shoes pulled free. Jeans in a faded denim puddle. Birgit took me on the bed, spread me out on the soft duvet, and started to speak German.

"What —?" I begged. "What did *you* say?" Now, I needed to know. I didn't want to miss any words.

"Relax," she told me, her body soft and warm on mine, curved and dipping in all the right places. She straddled my waist and looked down at me, then traced her fingertips along the line of my forehead, the bridge of my nose, before bringing them finally down to my mouth. Her fingertips rested on my lower lip and I drew them in, sucking on two, gently, softly.

I felt the place where our bodies were joined, felt the heat as it seemed to move from her to me. Felt the wetness when it started and I bucked up against her body, letting her know. But she knew. Easily, she moved down, kissing along the rise of my collarbones, down the hollow of my flat belly, making her way to the slicked wet split between my legs.

I thought of Johnny and wondered whether he was behind a smoked-glass door, making love to a stranger. I thought of the barker, offering nubile women for viewing pleasure, or more. And then I thought of nothing, as Birgit spread my nether lips wide open with her slippery fingers and brought her hot mouth against me. She touched my clit gingerly with the tip of her tongue, then ringed it with her parted lips. I felt the wealth of expertise in the way she touched me — she knew what she was doing. Her fingers came into play, holding my lips apart, dancing along the slick wet split. Then she moved her head down and her long hair tickled my inner thighs as she drew a line with her tongue from my pussy to my ass. I groaned and raised my hips, anxious to take whatever she would give.

Mouth glossy, she moved back and forth, licking and sliding, playing tricks and hide-and-seek games with her tongue deep inside of me. I turned my head and stared at the gold-painted wall, seeing our shadows there, growing and stretching with our movements. There were four of us in the room. Me and Birgit, and the two lovers on the wall. When I could take no more, I put my hands on her shoulders and made her look up at me. "Please –" I begged.

"What?" she asked, an echo, a murmur, "what did you say?"

"I want to taste you," I told her, and quickly she swivelled her lithe body around, so that her sex was poised and ready above my waiting mouth. Then we were connected again. My tongue inside her pussy, her whole face against my cunt, pressing hard. I didn't think. There was no need to. I only acted. Lips on her nether lips. Tongue flat to tickle her clit and then long and thin to thrust inside of her. I mimicked each move she made until we were in perfect rhythm. One beast, one being, riding together on that bed.

Nothing has ever felt that good, that right. The way we connected to one another. Skin sliding on skin. Fingers moving, caressing. Searching together to find the end – the answer.

With my eyes shut, I saw the women in the windows, the sluts under glass. With no sound but our hungry breaths, I heard the barker offer up his strippers, smooth and shaved, and then I was coming, and I heard only my heart in my ears as I drove hard against her mouth, sucked hard against her clit, taking her with me, taking her over.

Hours later, the boys found us curled in the bed together, me wearing one of Johnny's shirts, Birgit in one of Wolf's.

"Sleeping off a drunken night," chuckled Johnny knowingly as he and Wolf stumbled down the hall toward the tiny kitchen, where I could hear them trying, and failing, to be quiet as they looked for more alcohol. There was a loud bang and then Wolf groaned something in rapid-fire German.

"What did he say?" I asked Birgit, nuzzling my lips against her soft cheek.

"Nothing," she assured me, "nothing important." Her fingers once again found out the secret shaved skin of my bare pussy. Then quietly she spoke to me in German, and I closed my eyes and listened to the delicate murmurings of phrases that I knew meant promised pleasure, for once not worrying myself about the translation.

About the Author

Alison Tyler's erotic novels include *Learning To Love It, Strictly Confidential, Sweet Thing*, and the upcoming *Sticky Fingers*, all published by Black Lace Books. Two of her early novels, *The Blue Rose* and *The Virgin*, have recently been republished by Magic Carpet Books.

With Dante Davidson, she is the co-editor of the best-selling anthology *Bondage on a Budget*. Her short stories have appeared in anthologies including *Erotic Travel Tales I* and *II, Best Women's Erotica 2002* and *2003, Sweet Life, Best S/M Erotica, Guilty Pleasures, Sex Toy Tales, Best Lesbian Erotica 1996, Midsummer Night's Dreams,* and *Wicked Words 4, 5,* and *6*. Ms Tyler lives in the San Francisco Bay area, but she misses Los Angeles.